CLINT WAS JUST OUTSIDE OF HERMANN, MISSOURI, WHEN HE HEARD THE SHOTS.

There were a lot of them, too many for someone to just be taking target practice. From the looks of things five men had pinned down one lone man. Clint watched for a few moments as the men exchanged shots.

Clint removed his gun from his holster and checked to make sure all six cylinders were loaded. Next he checked his rifle. After that he took the reins in his teeth. Finally he saw four of the men stop to reload, and knew that this was his only chance. He kicked his horse on and started riding down on the men, firing as he went.

THE SPECIAL 200TH JUBILEE EDITION!

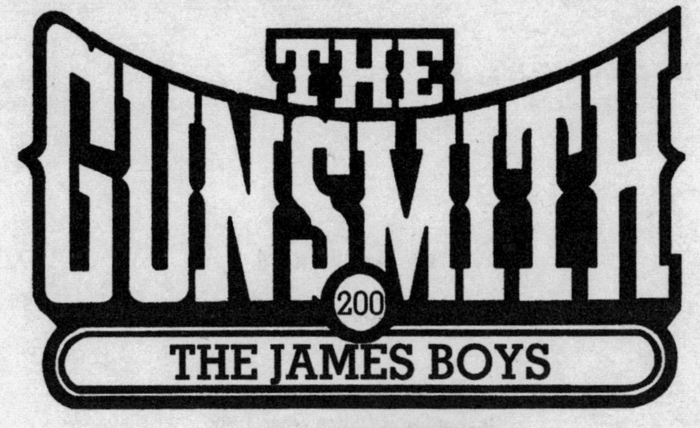

J. R. ROBERTS

JOVE BOOKS, NEW YORK

If you purchased this book without a cover, you should be aware that this book is stolen property. It was reported as "unsold and destroyed" to the publisher, and neither the author nor the publisher has received any payment for this "stripped book."

THE JAMES BOYS

A Jove Book / published by arrangement with
the author

PRINTING HISTORY
Jove edition / September 1998

The Penguin Putnam Inc. World Wide Web site address is
http://www.penguinputnam.com

ISBN: 0-515-12357-9

A JOVE BOOK®
Jove Books are published by The Berkley Publishing Group,
a member of Penguin Putnam Inc.,
200 Madison Avenue, New York, New York 10016.
JOVE and the "J" design are trademarks belonging to
Jove Publications, Inc.

PRINTED IN THE UNITED STATES OF AMERICA

10 9 8 7 6 5 4 3 2 1

PROLOGUE

Bob and Charley were nervous. They knew that if their target even suspected what they were up to, he'd kill them in a minute. In a fair fight they had no chance. Ten thousand dollars was plenty of incentive to come up with a plan that did not involve a fair fight.

"So, what do you boys think?" Mr. Howard asked. "Have you come to my home to tell me you'll join up?"

"Can't right say we come to a decision yet," Charley said. He was going to do the talking, and Bob was going to do the shooting. That was how they divvied up the plan. "After Northfield a man's gotta think twice."

"You don't have to worry about Northfield," Howard said. "If Cole and the others had listened to me it never would have happened—and nothin' like that is ever gonna happen again, not to any member of this gang."

Charley was wondering what to say to that when something amazing happened. Their host stretched his arms out, trying to relax, and then removed his guns and dropped the gun belt onto a nearby daybed. They couldn't believe their luck! With no guns he was an easy target.

Charley looked at Bob, who was supposed to do the deed, but Bob seemed frozen where he was.

"Charley? Bob? What's your answer gonna be?"

While he was waiting for their answer he looked up at a framed picture on the wall depicting the death of Stonewall Jackson. He frowned, looked around, picked up a nearby feather duster and pulled a chair over to the wall. He stood on the chair and started dusting the picture frame.

Charley Ford's eyes were popping as he looked at the man's back. He glared at his brother, whose heart was pounding so hard it felt like it was in his throat. Finally, Bob Ford stood up, drew his gun, and cocked his hammer.

On the chair, with his back to the Ford brothers, Jesse James knew he'd made a fatal error.

ONE

April 4, 1882

Clint Adams rode into St. Joseph, Missouri, and could feel the tension in the air. Something was happening in this town, and while he had no idea what it was, he knew it was something big enough to have affected everyone. There weren't that many people on the street, and those who were there followed him with wary eyes as he rode down the main street. Clint continued to ride, looking for the livery, and wondered where everyone was. Some of the stores were closed, and he wondered if it was some kind of local holiday.

Finally, when he reached the end of the street it broke off into two directions. From where he was he could see the livery was to his left, and he made for it, hoping that it, too, would not be closed. He wanted to get Duke taken care of so he could get a hotel room, a drink, a meal, and then a bath, in that order.

He rode Duke right up to the front of the livery and dismounted. One of the front doors was open, so he assumed it wasn't closed.

"Hello?" he called out. "Anyone here?"

He waited and was about to call out again when a young

man came running from the livery, tucking his shirt into his pants.

"Can you put up my horse?" Clint asked.

"Sure, but can you take 'im in yourself?" the young man asked. "I gotta go."

Clint took in the man's clothes, which were fairly dressy for a liveryman, and said, "You going to church or something? A wedding?"

"Ain't no wedding today, mister," the man said, doing his pants up. He appeared to be about nineteen, and in an almighty hurry.

"Where are you off to, then?"

"Mister, don't you know?" the young man asked. "I got to go to the inquest. You put your horse in any empty stall, and we can settle up later."

Clint was about to say something else, but the young man ran off before he could get it out.

"Something real strange is going on in this town, Duke," he said to the gelding. "Come on, let's get you taken care of."

He walked Duke into the livery, removed the saddle, took him into an empty stall and rubbed him down. Once that was done he made sure he had enough feed and then patted the big horse's neck.

"Well, that takes care of your needs," he said, "now to go and take care of mine."

He grabbed his saddlebags and rifle and left the livery, walking back toward the now almost deserted main street.

Whatever this inquest was that the young liveryman had told him about must have been real important to the town. He passed maybe three people as he walked back to where he had spotted the hotel earlier, and each was hurrying in the same direction as the others. All of the stores he passed were closed, and he worried that he wasn't going to be able to get something to eat.

It was almost three o'clock when he entered the hotel and presented himself at the desk. The clerk, a young man not much older than the liveryman, gave him an unhappy look.

"Yeah?"

"I'd like a room, if you don't mind."

"That's what I'm here for." The man turned the register around so Clint could sign in.

"And why are you here when nobody else seems to be working?" Clint asked as he signed in.

"Tell me about it," the clerk said, handing Clint a key. "I'm missing the biggest thing that ever happened in this town."

"Is that a fact? What's this inquest about, anyway?"

"You don't know? No, you wouldn't, you just got to town. Bob Ford, him and his brother, Charley, they shot Mr. Thomas Howard yesterday, shot and killed him."

"So they're the subject of the inquest?"

"That's right."

"And everybody knows they shot him?"

"Bob run through the streets, bragging about it. They done shot him right in the back."

Clint felt a coldness in his stomach.

"In the back? And that's something to brag about?"

"Yes, sir," the clerk said, "and they's gonna collect a ten thousand dollar reward, once the inquest is over."

"How are they going to spend that money if they're in jail?"

"Oh, they ain't going to jail," the man said, "everybody knows that. Bob, he says he made a deal with T. T. Crittenden hisself."

"The governor made a deal with these men to shoot another man in the back?"

"Yes, sir."

Clint frowned.

"Thomas Howard?" he asked. "I don't believe I know the name."

"Weren't his real name, that's why," the man said. "Nobody in town knew it 'til yesterday."

"What was his real name, then?"

"Why, he was Jesse James!"

TWO

Clint wasn't sure he'd heard right.

"Say that again?"

"The Ford brothers," the clerk said, "they killed Jesse James."

"That's what I thought you said. And they shot him in the back?"

"Do you know any other way to kill Jesse James, Mister—" The clerk turned the book around and read Clint's name. It was clear from his reaction that he recognized it.

"Holy—ain't you the Gunsmith?"

"Where are the Fords now?"

"At the inquest, I guess. They was in jail overnight, but everybody knew they wouldn't stay there."

"And you say they made a deal with the governor?"

"That's what Bob's been sayin'. There's some stuff about it all in today's paper, too."

"What's the local paper?"

"Ain't got one. The closest we got is the Carrollton *Democrat*. They brung copies over here right early."

"Have you got one?"

"Sure do," the clerk said, producing it from under the desk. "Plan on keeping it, ya know, for prosperity, or whatever they say—hey!"

Clint had grabbed the paper from the man's grasp.

"I'll give it back. Where's this inquest being held?"

"In the courthouse, down the street a couple of blocks."

"When's it supposed to start?"

"Three o'clock."

Clint looked at the clock on the wall behind the desk, which said it was five after.

"Take my rifle and my saddlebags to my room, will you?"

"Sure thing, Mr. Adams, sure thing, but—"

Clint turned and walked out without giving the young man a chance to speak further.

"Gawdamn it," he said, "the Gunsmith is going to the Jesse James inquest, and I'm stuck here!"

Clint entered the courtroom and saw that it was standing room only. Several people had to move away from the door to allow him to enter, and he was barely able to find a space against the wall to stand.

"Who's on the stand?" he asked the person next to him.

"That there's Charley Ford," an elderly man said.

"The one whose brother shot Jesse?"

"T'warn't Jesse," the old man said. "Whole thing's a put-up job."

A man on Clint's right nodded his agreement.

Clint listened first to Charley Ford's testimony. Ford argued that people were saying the dead man wasn't Jesse, but he'd known Jesse a long time and it was him.

"He used to come over to the house when I was on my oldest brother's farm," Charley Ford said. "Then he moved here and started living under the name Thomas Howard."

He went on to tell how he and his brother Bob had gone to Jesse's house, that Jesse thought they were considering joining his gang, but they were just waiting for their chance to pull down on him. They were surprised when that chance came, because Jesse removed his guns and tossed them on his bed.

"As he turned from the bed we stepped between him and his guns and pulled down on him."

He described in detail how they shot him and where each bullet had gone. It took Clint a while, but he finally located Jesse's mother and his wife, Zee, who were sitting together, holding hands.

Clint noticed something odd. Both of the Ford boys were armed. He assumed this could not have been an oversight on the part of the sheriff, so apparently they had been given permission.

After Charley finished, his brother Bob took the stand. Clint was surprised at how young and slight Bob Ford looked. He described how he had come to know Jesse and members of his gang without ever having joined them, and backed up his brother's story about how they shot him. Afterward, he said, they went and sent wires to the governor, to Police Commissioner Craig, and to Sheriff Timberlake. Clint was surprised that so many men in authority were in on this.

They all testified that day, except the governor, who was not in attendance. Commissioner Craig—who hadn't known Jesse—said his piece, and Sheriff Timberlake—who claimed he had known Jesse—said his. When it was all over the finding was that Jesse James came to his death by a wound in the head intentionally fired by Robert Ford. Afterward Clint was surprised when both Ford boys were arrested and charged with the murder of Jesse James, on an affidavit sworn out by Mrs. Jesse James. However, as Charley and Bob were led from the courtroom Clint noticed that neither of them looked particularly worried. He wondered if it had ever occurred to them that Governor Crittenden might have lied to them and intended for them to either go to jail or be executed for killing Jesse James.

No, from what Clint knew of Crittenden, it was more likely that the politician had made a deal with the Ford boys to once and for all get rid of a major thorn in his side.

After the Fords left, followed by both the police commissioner and the sheriff, the spectators started to file out. Clint maintained his position against the wall, out of the way of the crowd that flowed through the door like a tidal wave he didn't want to get caught up in.

And then they were coming up the aisle, Jesse's mother, Zerelda Samuels, and his wife, also Zerelda but called Zee. Zee was holding Jesse's mother's arm, but Clint doubted that the older woman needed the support. It was more likely Zee was seeking support than giving it. Still, it was Zee who saw him first.

"Clint."

"Zee."

"Mother James, it's Clint—"

"I see him, child," Zerelda James Samuels said. "Clint, they killed my boy, they killed him!"

"I know, Mother James, I know."

And then she was in his arms and crying on his chest, and it all came flooding back to Clint, how he'd first met the James boys and their family back in the spring of '73. . . .

THREE

1873 MISSOURI

Clint was just outside of Hermann, Missouri, when he heard the shots. There were a lot of them, too many for someone to just be taking target practice. He reined his horse in and stood in the stirrups for a moment until he thought he had the direction the shots were coming from. Knowing that a smart man would have ridden the other way, he nevertheless rode in the direction of the shots.

He topped a rise and stopped, looking down at the meadow that sprawled out ahead of him. This was where the shots were coming from all right. From the looks of things five men had pinned down one lone man. They were using some rocks for cover, while he looked to be lying in a gully of some sort. Clint watched for a few moments as the men exchanged shots. The pinned man was economical with his, while the other five just kept firing away, trying to get lucky. They had to stop every so often to reload, and the longer he watched the more he realized that, sooner or later, the timing was going to work so that the five men were overlapping in their reloading—and they might even all have to reload at the same time.

Clint removed his gun from his holster and checked to

make sure all six cylinders were loaded. Next he checked his rifle. After that he took the reins in his teeth, knowing that it was more likely than anything that he'd fall off his horse, but he once saw an overweight marshal with an eye patch do the same thing, and it worked then.

He waited for the timing to be right. He knew he wouldn't be able to fire accurately with the rifle, but it was more important that he make a lot of noise than truly hit anything.

He watched, and waited, and hoped that the pinned down man wouldn't catch a stray bullet while he was waiting. Finally, he saw four of the men stop to reload, and knew that this was his only chance. He spurred his horse on—kicked him on, since he wore no spurs—and started riding down on the men, firing as he went.

He didn't know what the fight was about, who was right or who was wrong, he just knew that five men were attacking one, and those weren't very good odds, no matter what the lone man had done.

He was firing with both hands, and the reins in his mouth felt as if they would pull his teeth out. The four men who were in the act of reloading looked up the hill and saw this crazy man riding down on them.

The pinned down man did his part, standing up at that point and firing as quickly as he could. The five men realized they were suddenly caught in a cross fire, and had not reloaded yet. They did the only thing that seemed prudent—they ran for their horses.

The fifth man, however, not having to reload, decided to throw a couple of shots at Clint as he ran for his mount, and Clint felt the horse stagger beneath him and knew that the animal had been hit. The animal courageously kept his feet, however, until the five men had mounted and ridden off. Clint holstered his gun and grabbed the reins with his hand, hoping to control the animal and keep him from injuring himself further, but before he could take action the animal went to his knees, and then keeled over. Clint barely had time to throw himself free so that he wouldn't be pinned by the dead horse.

He hit the ground hard but got to his feet quickly to turn and look at the animal. He was just in time to see the light go out in the horse's eye.

"A damned shame," someone said behind him.

He turned, ready to defend himself, but the man held out both hands to show that he was unarmed at the moment.

"He was a fine-looking animal," the man said. "I'm sorry you lost him by coming to my aid."

"It's a fair trade," Clint said. "A man's life for a horse."

"It's kind of you to say so," the man said. He was tall, lanky, with a two-or three-day growth of stubble on his lean jaw. He appeared to be twenty-seven or -eight, maybe older.

"Allow me to introduce myself so you know who you traded your horse for," the man said, extending his hand. Clint took it as the man spoke his name. "Frank James."

"A pleasure to meet you," Clint said, releasing the outlaw's hand.

"Do you know the name?"

"I know it."

"Aren't you . . ."

"What? Impressed? Reputations don't impress me. What you did, there, at the end, though, that impressed me."

"What did I do?"

"You stood up and abandoned your cover to help me."

"You helped me," James said. "It seemed only fair."

Frank James walked over to the fallen horse.

"Had him long?" he asked.

"Not long," Clint said. "A few months."

"Name him?"

"He came with a name," Clint said. "Pecos."

Frank considered the name for a few moments, then said, "Damned fool name for a horse. What was he, three, four?"

"Four."

"Looks part Arabian."

"You have a good eye."

Frank James shrugged and turned to face Clint, the dead horse forgotten.

"My horses are in that stand of trees, far back from where I was taking cover. I didn't want them taking a stray bullet."

"Horses?"

Frank nodded.

"I have an extra. You can use him if you like, until we get where we're going."

"Are we going somewhere?"

"To Hermann."

"What for?"

"Dinner," Frank said. "It's the least I can do for the man who saved my life. You can meet my brother, and we'll see about getting you a horse to replace this one. Come on, together we can get your saddle off of him."

"Appreciate the help."

"Like I said," Frank replied, "I owe you. By the way, I didn't catch your name."

"I didn't give it," Clint said. "It's Adams, Clint Adams."

Frank was turning toward the horse when Clint said his name, and the man stopped short, obviously recognizing it.

"Well, if that don't beat all," he finally said, laughing. "That explains why you weren't impressed by my reputation, don't it?"

"Does it make a difference?" Clint asked.

"It surely does, Clint—can I call you Clint?"

"Why not?"

"Why not, indeed? Well, I tell you, friend Clint, it makes a difference who you are, but not in any way you'd understand right now. Let's get this saddle off your horse and head for Hermann. I think Jesse's gonna be happy to meet you."

FOUR

"The bank," Clint said.

"What?"

"The bank in St. Genevieve," Clint said to Frank James. "That was you and your brother, wasn't it?"

Frank James almost blushed. They'd been riding awhile, Clint sitting this new horse uncomfortably. It was a young animal, not one of a size, and he usually liked bigger horses. He wondered how long it would take him, this time, to find one that fit him.

"Not just me and Jesse, but yeah, it was us."

"So was that a posse I was shooting at back there? I mean, I'd like to know if I was shooting at some lawmen."

"No, not a posse," Frank said, "just some boys who recognized me and thought they'd take me for the reward money."

"I thought you fellas had all of Missouri on your side."

"Well," Frank said, "I guess they weren't from Missouri."

"And what's in Hermann?" Clint asked. "Another bank?"

"No," Frank said, "just dinner. Why? Have you got something against bank robbing?"

"Bank robbing and train robbing," Clint said, "are not

things I would choose to do for a living, but if that's what you and your brother want to do, then go ahead.''

''It's not what we want to do,'' Frank said, ''it's what we have to do.''

Clint held up his hand to keep Frank from saying anything more.

''Spare me the details,'' he said. ''I've read all the stories about you and your brother, and your battle with the railroad.''

''And do you believe those stories?''

''I'm not a man who believes everything I hear,'' Clint said, ''or everything I read.''

''I didn't think you would be,'' Frank said, ''not a man with a reputation like yours. Why'd you stop bein' a lawman?''

''The job stopped agreeing with me.''

''Ever think of moving to the other side?''

''Are you asking me to join your gang?''

''No,'' Frank said, ''I'd have to talk that over with Jesse first.''

They rode in silence a little while longer and then Frank said, ''That horse don't suit you, does it?''

''Not particularly.''

''We'll have to see about gettin' you a new one.''

''I usually take care of buying my own horses.''

Frank laughed and asked, ''Who was talkin' about buyin'?''

When they rode into Hermann there was no posse waiting for them. Frank commented on this.

''Were you expecting one?''

''There was a chance,'' Frank said, ''especially since Jesse left a note sayin' we'd be eatin' dinner here.''

''What?''

Frank chuckled.

''He does things like that, sometimes.''

''Why?''

"Who knows?" Frank said. "He's a little crazy, Jesse is—but don't ever say that to his face."

"Don't worry," Clint said, "I won't."

They rode down Market Street to the livery stable in Hermann and put their horses up there. Clint knew a little about Hermann, mainly that it had been settled by Germans. This was obvious from the names on some of the storefronts. Also, when the liveryman came out to greet them, he had a German accent.

"Ve haff visitors," the man said. "*Ja, gut.*"

Frank laughed at the man's accent, an enjoyable sound, not a derisive one. Clint claimed his saddle from the borrowed animal and set it aside. He asked the man about horses for sale and was told there were some in the back. Clint said he'd come back later and have a look. At that moment he wanted to get a room and then a meal.

As they left the livery Frank said, "Didn't see Jesse's horse in there, or any of the others. Guess they haven't got here yet."

"How did you get separated?"

"Oh, we did that after St. Genevieve. It just makes it harder on a posse."

"How hard could it be when you tell them where you're going to be for dinner?"

"Yeah," Frank said, "but do they believe us?"

The two men went to the Hermannhaus Hotel and got rooms. Clint decided to go to his room for a while. Frank said he'd come and get him for dinner when Jesse and the others got there.

"You're gonna want to meet Jesse."

Clint wasn't sure about that, but he didn't turn down the offer. After all, Frank wanted to do something for the man who'd saved his life.

In his room Clint walked to the window that overlooked Market Street and wondered what he was getting himself into—and why? He'd left enforcing the law behind for a life of traveling. Yet here he was in Hermann with one of the James boys, waiting for the other one to arrive with the rest of the gang. There was a time when he would have arrested them on the spot. Now he was waiting to have dinner with all of them.

Life got strange sometimes.

FIVE

Jesse James rode into Hermann, Missouri, an hour later with Bill Chadwell and Clell Miller in tow. Cole and Bob Younger had not yet arrived. The three men rode directly to the livery and handed their horses over to the German liveryman. As they turned to walk back to Market Street, Jesse saw his brother Frank walking toward him with a big smile on his face.

"You boys go on ahead," Jesse said to Chadwell and Miller. "Get yourselves a room."

"I'm for gettin' a drink first," Chadwell said.

"I'm with you on that," Miller said.

"Suit yourselves."

Miller and Chadwell exchanged greetings with Frank as they all passed each other. When Frank reached Jesse, the two young men embraced.

"Good to see you, Dingus," Frank said to his younger brother.

"Frank," Jesse said, releasing his brother. "Didn't see Cole's and Bob's horses."

"They're not here yet."

"You have any trouble when we split up?"

"Some," Frank said. "Some fellas tried to collect on the price on my head."

"Doesn't look like they got it," Jesse said, making a show of examining his brother's head.

"Well, not for not trying," Frank said. "There was five of them, and they had me pinned down good."

They turned and started walking toward Market Street together.

"How'd you get away?"

"With help."

"From who?"

"You'll never guess."

"I don't want to guess."

"The Gunsmith."

Jesse stopped walking.

"Clint Adams?"

"That's right."

"Why'd he help you?"

"Why not? Anyway, he didn't know it was me until after we chased the five of them off."

"And then what?"

"And then I brought him here."

Jesse looked sharply at his brother.

"Why'd you do that?"

"To buy him dinner," Frank said. "Least I could do after he lost his horse saving my life."

"His horse?"

"Caught a stray bullet, went down."

"You had that extra mount with you."

"I did," Frank said, "and I let him use it. Doesn't suit him, though. He needs somethin' bigger."

"Sounds like you want to get him a horse."

"I wouldn't mind," Frank said. "A meal don't hardly seem enough of a payback."

"Probably not," Jesse said. "Ma'd be pretty mad if we didn't pay him back."

"I know it."

"Where is he?"

"At the hotel. I told him I'd come and get him when you got here."

"And what makes you think he ain't after us, Frank?"

"He ain't a lawman no more, Jess."

"What about the reward?"

"I ain't never heard anything about him bein' a bounty hunter."

"So what was he doin' out there, near St. Genevieve?"

"He says he was just passin'."

"And you want to take him at his word?"

"I do."

They walked a bit more, toward the hotel, and then Jesse said, "Reckon I can't argue none with you. Bring 'im to dinner and let's meet him."

"We gonna wait for Cole and Bob to eat?"

"Naw," Jesse said. "Any sign of the law?"

"No," Frank said. "I guess nobody wanted to take us up on our invitation."

"Go get your new friend, then," Jesse said, "and let's eat."

SIX

When the knock came at the door Clint knew he had gone too far now to quit. When he opened the door he saw Frank in the hall.

"Jesse's here," he said. "Let's eat."

As it turned out Jesse had picked Hermann as a place for them to have dinner because he liked German food. Clint couldn't recall having eaten German food before, but as they entered the restaurant the smells that assailed his nostrils were delicious.

Frank led him to a table where a man was sitting alone. He was younger than Frank, that was obvious, and his hair was lighter, but it was also obvious they were brothers. Both were tall and slender, and not particularly dangerous-looking—in a restaurant.

"Jesse, meet Clint Adams," Frank said, making the introductions. "Clint, my brother, Jesse."

Jesse stood and shook hands with Clint, a good, solid handshake.

"I heard a lot about you," he said, "and not just from Frank."

"Same here."

"I want to thank you for saving Frank's life. I'm kinda used to havin' him around."

"Seemed like the thing to do at the time."

"Sit down. Frank?"

The three of them sat.

"I thought there'd be more men with you," Clint said.

"Clell and Bill are gonna eat somewheres else," Jesse said. "They ain't fond of German food. Cole and Bob ain't got here yet."

"The Youngers."

"That's right," Jesse said. "Reckon they'll be along later. I'm too hungry to wait for them, though."

"Me, too," Frank said.

"Ever had German food before?" Jesse asked Clint.

"Can't say I have."

"It's real good," Jesse said. "Sticks to the ribs. We've eaten here before, and the food's real good."

"Why don't I leave it to you boys to order, then?" Clint asked.

"We'll do that," Jesse said, exchanging nods with Frank. He called the waiter over and ordered, and Clint heard "braten" and "schnitzel" and didn't know what either one was. He didn't much care, either, at that moment. All he could think of was that he was sitting in a restaurant with Frank and Jesse James, and if they knew why he was there, they'd probably try to kill him rather than feed him.

SEVEN

Dinner turned out to be different kinds of meats in heavy sauces, which Clint found delicious. In fact, the food was so good he stopped thinking about the James boys killing him. The beer was also German, heavy and dark, and when it came to the coffee it was just the way he liked it, hot and black. Dessert was something called "apple strudel," and he almost asked for another one.

After dinner Jesse sat back and rubbed his stomach.

"I know how you feel," Clint said. "I'm stuffed."

"I told you," Jesse said, "this kind of food sticks to your ribs."

"I got to walk this off," Frank said. "I'm gonna see if Cole and Bob got here yet."

"Okay, you do that," Jesse said. "Clint and I will get better acquainted. We'll see you at the saloon. You know which one."

"Right."

Frank left and Clint poured himself some more coffee from the pot. When he held it up to Jesse, the younger man shook his head.

"My brother wants to do something for you, for saving his life."

"It's not necessary."

"Yes, it is," Jesse said. "I feel the same way, and my ma would, too. She always told us to pay our debts, and we owe you a big one."

"Jesse . . ."

"I want you to come to my weddin'."

That surprised Clint.

"What?"

"I'm gettin' married a year from now," Jesse said. "I'm invitin' you to come."

"A year from now."

"April twenty-fourth, next year. Will you come?"

"Well, Jesse," Clint said, "I don't rightly know where I'll be a year from now."

"I do." Jesse had been sitting back in his chair, with the front legs up off the ground, and now he sat forward so that the legs met the floor with a bang. The look in his eyes changed and suddenly he did look like the man Clint had heard about and read about. He looked dangerous. "You'll be at my ma's house, for my weddin'."

Clint didn't see any point in arguing now over something that was going to happen in a year.

"All right, Jesse," he said, "I'll be there."

"Good," Jesse said, " 'cause Ma's gonna want to thank you, too, and I'll be wantin' you to meet my Zee. That's Zerelda, she's gonna be my wife."

"I'll look forward to it."

"Good," Jesse said. He smiled and that look faded from his eyes. "Now, why don't we go and meet Frank and see if he found Cole and Bob."

"Sure," Clint said, "why not?"

When they got to the saloon Frank was already there. He was with Clell Miller, Bill Chadwell, and the Youngers, Bob and Cole. Jesse and Clint joined them, and Jesse made the introductions. The other men regarded Clint curiously, and suspiciously, but they didn't say anything in front of him.

The saloon at that time of day was usually pretty full, but

although the people of Hermann had nothing against the James-Younger gang, neither did they want to be around them in case a posse showed up and some shooting started. For that reason the seven men had the place to themselves, except for the four girls who worked there.

One of the girls tried to sit in Jesse's lap, but he shooed her away. After all, he was getting married next year. Instead she went to Clint, who had no problem with her sitting on him. She was a solidly built blonde with big breasts, and her butt felt real nice pressed into his lap. The other three girls settled on Frank and the Youngers, making both Chadwell and Miller pretty unhappy. They spent most of the evening glaring at Clint, as if it was his fault they didn't have a girl. As far as Clint was concerned one of them could have her later, because he hadn't paid for sex before and he didn't intend to on that night. As it turned out, he didn't have to worry about paying, but he didn't know that then.

It became apparent to him, as Miller and Chadwell treated him with less and less respect, that they thought, because they rode with Jesse James, they didn't need to fear or respect anyone else.

Things came to a head when Clell Miller reached over and grabbed the blonde's arm.

"Hey, Bettina," he said, "how about comin' over and warmin' my lap for a change?"

"No," she said in slightly accented English. She put her arms around Clint's neck. "I like it here."

Clint liked her there, too, especially with her fleshy arms around his neck. It brought her scented bosom even closer to him. He wondered idly if he could get her to come to his room for the night, for free.

"Hey, how about it, Adams?" Miller said. "You gonna share?"

"Find your own girl, Miller," Clint said, putting his arm around Bettina's waist. "The girl wants to stay with me."

"There's only four girls in the whole place," Miller snapped.

"There's a whole town out there," Clint said. "Have a look."

Miller looked at Chadwell, who nodded. Frank and Jesse saw what was going on and sat back to watch. Cole and Bob were drinking and didn't notice anything.

Miller stood up slowly.

"I say she comes with me, now."

"And I say that's up to her," Clint said, "isn't it?"

"I'm makin' the decision for her," Miller said, and grabbed her arm again, this time with his left hand, which made his intention fairly clear.

"Hey, ow!" the girl cried out.

Miller had outsmarted himself. Reaching for the girl left-handed he got in his own way, but it really didn't matter. No matter how he did it he still would have been looking down the barrel of Clint's gun as he went to draw his.

Miller stopped short, his gun still in his holster. He didn't understand how Clint could have read him, let alone drawn his gun so fast.

"You feel tense over there, Chadwell," Clint said. "Why don't you relax while I talk to your friend, here."

Chadwell, whose own hand had been inching toward his gun, decided to take the advice. He had never seen anyone draw a gun so fast. In fact, that was the trouble. He never even *saw* Clint Adams draw.

"Bettina, you'd better move aside for now, sweetheart," Clint said, and the girl obeyed.

"You want to die for a woman, Miller?" Clint asked.

Miller was still staring at Clint's gun.

"I'll holster my gun and you can try again. I won't even stand up. But this time," Clint said, cocking the hammer back, "I'll fire, instead of just cocking the gun."

Slowly he eased the hammer down, then holstered the weapon.

"Go ahead, Miller," Clint said, "make your choice."

All eyes were on Clell Miller, which didn't help the situation any.

"Jesse?"

"What, Clell?"

Miller tore his eyes away from Clint and looked at Jesse. "You gonna let him get away with this?"

"It's between you and him, Clell," Jesse said. "He asks a good question, though. *Do* you want to die for a woman?"

"Frank?" Miller said.

"Don't look at me, Clell," Frank said. "You started it."

"Cole? Bob?"

"Huh?" they both said.

Miller glared at Chadwell, who was supposed to have backed his play.

"I'll give you another choice, Clell," Clint said, drawing the man's attention again.

"What's that?"

"Sit back down and I'll buy you a drink."

Miller was sweating, and the perspiration was making his underarms itch and smell.

"Sounds like a good idea to me, Clell," Jesse said.

Clell Miller licked his lips and then said to Clint, "I ain't drinkin' with you."

"Then get out," Clint said.

Miller looked at the others again, then left the saloon in a hurry.

"Billy," Jesse said, "go with him and make sure he don't get in any trouble."

"Sure, Jesse."

Chadwell rose, eyed Clint warily, then walked after Clell Miller.

"Thanks for not killin' him," Jesse said. "It would have taken me a while to replace him."

"I'm not about to kill a man over a woman," Clint said, then looked hurriedly at Bettina. "No offense."

"I won't be offended," she said, "if you let me come back to your lap."

Clint spread his arms and said, "I'm all ready for you."

EIGHT

Cole and Bob Younger left the saloon sometime later, leaving Clint there with the James boys.

"What's their problem?" Clint asked.

Some other customers had finally gotten brave enough to come into the saloon now that the whole gang wasn't there, and Bettina had gone off to do her job.

"Cole and Bob are suspicious," Frank said.

Jesse laughed and said, "Clell and Billy just don't like you a whole lot, Clint."

"That's okay," Clint said. "I can live with that."

"Well, maybe not," Jesse said, "but I'll make sure they don't come after you. I wouldn't want them to kill you, or you to kill them—not until after my weddin', anyway. Frank, I'm gonna turn in. We want to get an early start come morning."

"Sure, Jess," Frank said. "I'll be along directly."

"Clint, I'll look forward to seein' you again."

Clint stood and shook hands with Jesse James, then watched him walk out of the saloon.

"So, what do you think?"

Clint told the truth.

"He's real likeable."

"Yeah, he is."

"But he's changeable, too."

"Oh, you saw that, huh?"

"It's in his eyes."

"Yeah, it is," Frank said. "Quantrill once told me that if what's inside Jess ever came out, there'd be hell to pay."

"So you look after him."

Frank shrugged.

"He's my brother," Frank said. "You must know what that's like, to look after somebody."

"Afraid I don't," Clint said. "I never had a brother."

"You got friends."

"A few."

"One or two that maybe you're as close to as if you were brothers?"

Clint thought a moment about Wild Bill Hickok and said, "Maybe."

"Then you understand."

Clint didn't reply.

"I'm going back to the hotel."

"I'll walk over with you," Clint said. "I want to get an early start looking at horses in the morning."

They got up and started walking to the doors. Before they got there, though, the doors opened and five men walked in. Clint instinctively knew that these were the five men he had saved Frank from earlier.

"Shit," Frank said.

The five men took one look at Frank and went for their guns, leaving Frank and Clint no choice. They both drew and the shooting started. When it was all over the five men lay dead on the saloon floor. Clint had killed three, Frank two.

"You know," Frank said, "I ain't never seen anybody shoot the way you do—except maybe for Jesse."

"You'd better get out of here," Clint said. "The shooting's going to attract the law."

"What are you gonna tell 'em?"

"That I killed all five."

Frank chuckled.

"That'll add to your reputation."

"What about the others in here, though?" Clint asked.

Frank looked around at the few men who were still in the place, and the bartender.

"Don't worry," Frank said, "they won't say nothin' about me."

"Get going then," Clint said. "I'll handle this."

"Looks like you saved my bacon again, Clint," Frank said. "I'm gonna owe you for a long time. A real long time. . . ."

NINE

St. Joseph, Missouri
April 4, 1882

Zerelda Samuels and Zee James—or Howard—insisted that Clint come to the house with them, the house Jesse was killed in. When they got there Zee put on some water for coffee, and Zerelda just sat at the kitchen table, shaking her head.

"I can't believe my boy's gone," she said.

"What about Frank?" Clint asked. "Where is he? Does he know about Jesse?"

"He knows," Zee said. "He's far from here."

"He's going to go after the Fords," Clint said.

"He's a fool if he does," Zee said. "The Fords had the blessing of the governor. They'll be in jail for a while, but only to protect them. And when they get out they'll be watched. The law will be waiting for Frank to make a move on them."

"What about the rest of the gang?"

"There is no rest," Zee said. "The days of the James gang were just about over, Clint. Jesse was talking to Charley and Bob about joining, but I knew they never would. They—" She stopped short, laughing.

"What's funny, Zee?" Jesse's mother asked.

"I was going to say they didn't have the balls to join Jesse, but I guess they had the balls to kill him, huh?"

"It doesn't take courage to shoot a man in the back," Clint said, thinking of Jack McCall and Wild Bill Hickok. This made three friends he had lost to a coward's bullet.

"When are they going to let you have Jesse?" Clint asked.

Zee brought three cups of coffee to the table and sat down.

"At first they refused to turn him over to us," Zee said, "but a telegram from the governor changed that. We'll get him tomorrow."

"What will you do with . . . with his body?"

"Take it home to Kearney," Jesse's mother said, "and bury him in the front yard."

"That's where we'll see Frank," Zee said.

"I'll meet you here in the morning," Clint said. "I want to make sure you get him on that train with no trouble."

Mrs. Samuels reached across the table and took Clint's hand.

"I'm mighty glad you're here, Clint," she said. "You saved my boys' lives more than once. It's fitting you should be here."

He placed his hand over hers and said, "I'm glad I'm here, too."

"How did you hear about it so soon?" Zee asked.

"I didn't," Clint said. "I didn't even know you and Jesse were here under the name Howard."

"You just rode in by coincidence?" she asked. "You hate coincidences. I remember that about you."

"Well, they happen," Clint said. "There's nothing I can do about this one."

Clint studied Zee James. She had become a beautiful woman during the years he hadn't seen her. Now, unfortunately, not yet thirty, she had become a beautiful widow.

"I'd better have a look around town," Clint said, "see if there's any trouble brewing. Is there anyone in town who would help?"

"Ben Morrow and Sim Whitsett are in town," Zee said. "They served under Quantrill with Jesse."

"I'll find them," Clint said.

"I'll walk you out," Zee said. She touched her mother-in-law's shoulder as she passed her. "I'll be right back, Mother."

Clint and Zee walked to the front door. There was a crowd of people outside.

"Looking for souvenirs," Zee said. "Ghouls."

"You want me to send them on their way?"

"No," Zee said wearily, "they'd just come back after you'd gone."

Clint looked Zee in the eyes.

"You don't look cried out, Zee."

"I haven't cried yet, Clint," she said. "Maybe once we get Jesse on the train the tears will come."

"Zee," he said, putting a hand on her shoulder, "I'm so sorry . . ."

"I know, Clint, I know," she said. "Could I ask you something? A favor?"

"Anything."

"Don't say that until you hear what it is."

"Okay."

"Would come with us, to Kearney? To bury Jesse?"

"Sure," he said. "I'd be happy to."

"And would you talk to Frank?"

"About what?"

"He's going to be real upset for a long time, Clint," she said. "He and Jesse, they weren't on the best terms, and now that Jesse's dead they can't make it right—and Jesse wanted to, so desperately."

"Then maybe you should tell Frank that."

"I intend to," she said, "but Frank and Jesse, they respected you. He'd listen to you, Clint."

"I'll try, Zee," Clint said. "I'll come with you and sure give it a try."

"Thank you, Clint," she said. "Thank you."

TEN

Clint found Morrow and Whitsett in one of the town saloons, having their own private little wake. He vaguely remembered meeting the men at Jesse's wedding, and when he introduced himself to them they remembered him and greeted him warmly as a friend of Jesse and Frank.

"I'll get you a beer," Whitsett said, and went to the bar before Clint could stop him.

"When did you get to town?" Morrow asked. He was about Jesse's age, thirty-four or -five, short and stocky, while the lanky Whitsett was a little older.

"Just today," Clint said. "I didn't know what I was riding into."

"It's a damned shame," Morrow said. "Those damned Fords."

"Do we know which one actually pulled the trigger?" Clint asked. "From the inquest it sounded like both of them."

"Bob did it," Morrow said, "we know that for a fact. And I'll tell you something. We're gonna get him for it."

Clint remembered that neither Whitsett—who returned now with his beer—nor Morrow were ever part of Jesse's gang. Clint doubted that either of them had broken the law, or killed a man since the war.

"Forget about Bob for now," Clint said. "I need your help with something."

"Name it," Morrow said.

Briefly, Clint told them how Jesse's family wanted to get him to the train so they could take him home and bury him.

"I'll need help making sure they get to that train," he finished.

"I'll be there," Morrow said.

"Me, too," Whitsett said.

"I knew I could count on you boys," Clint said.

He stayed long enough to remember Jesse while they finished their beers, and when he got up to leave Morrow asked him, "You still got that horse? The big gelding?"

"Still got him," Clint said.

"Must be eight or nine by now."

"Nine," Clint said, "and still going strong."

"You were surprised when Jesse give you that horse," Whitsett said.

"Yeah," Clint said, recalling that day, "I sure was surprised, all right."

He went back to his hotel and waited until he was in his room before he allowed himself the luxury of thinking back. . . .

ELEVEN

JESSE JAMES'S WEDDING DAY, 1874

Clint had no idea how Jesse knew where he was, but he received a telegram telling him that the wedding was in three days—April 24—and that they were expecting him to be there.

The telegram reached him in Denver, where Clint had gone to report to Allan Pinkerton. Had Jesse and Frank known that he was working for Pinkerton when he met them, they surely would have killed him. He wasn't actually a Pinkerton, but he did some jobs for them from time to time. This was the last, however. That's what he was telling Allan. He and the famous detective never got along, and as far as Clint was concerned they had gone as far as they could go.

In fact, they'd had their last meeting that morning, before he got the telegram.

"And I'll tell you something else," Allan had said to him in his office. "I still think you lied to me last year about the James boys."

"Why would I lie?" Clint asked. "I never saw them."

"Then I paid you good money for nothing," Pinkerton said. "You're not the man I thought you were."

"I guess not."

"Hogwash!"

How could he tell Allan that he had not only met the James boys, but had saved Frank James's life twice? And he hadn't saved Frank just to turn him over to the Pinkertons. On top of everything else, he'd ended up liking those boys.

"Allan, you and I just don't see eye to eye," Clint said. "I don't think I'll be taking any work from you anymore."

"Well, that's fine," Pinkerton said, "because I wasn't going to give you any more."

This sounded like a reverse you-can't-fire-me-I-quit routine that Clint didn't want to play.

"Fine."

"And I should let you take your friend Roper with you, too."

"Talbot Roper is the best man you have," Clint said. "You're a fool if you let him go."

"He's as irresponsible and arrogant as you are."

"He's more arrogant than me," Clint said, "because he knows how good a detective he is."

"Not a team player," said the older man. "Not at all. We need team players."

"If you ask me," Clint said, "you've got too many damned team players and not enough good men like Roper."

"Well, I didn't ask you," Pinkerton said. "Get out of my office."

"I'm going, Allan."

"And that's another thing!" Pinkerton shouted as Clint went through the door. "I never said you could call me Allan!"

Clint stood in the lobby of his hotel—the Denver House—and read the invitation to Jesse James's wedding, wondering what Pinkerton would say if he knew.

"From a lady?"

He looked up and saw Talbot Roper approaching.

"An invitation to a wedding," he said, pocketing the telegram. He had not even told his friend Roper about the meeting with the James boys.

"Not yours, I hope."

"No, no, not mine."

"And I know it's not mine."

"No."

"And you're not going to tell me whose it is, are you?" Roper asked.

"No," Clint said, "you're the great detective. You find out."

"If I cared," Roper said, "I would. Ready to eat?"

"Let's go."

They went into the hotel dining room and were seated.

"What'd you do to the old bear today?" Roper asked. "He was growling more than usual."

"Did he fire you?"

"No," Roper said, "should I expect to be fired, thank you very much?"

"That's up to you, I guess."

"I don't think he'll have time to fire me," Roper said. "I'm going to quit and open my own shop."

"Good for you."

"Why don't you come in with me?" Roper asked. "We could be partners."

"I'm not a detective."

"That's okay," Roper said, "I'm detective enough for both of us. I just need somebody I can talk to."

"Get a dog."

"That's an idea," Roper said.

They ordered dinner and sat back to wait.

"When are you going to tell him?"

"Next week," Roper said. "I'm still looking for an office. When are you leaving town?"

"Tomorrow," Clint said. "The wedding's in three days, and I've got to get there in time."

"Well, do me a favor," Roper said.

"What?"

"Give my best to the groom," Roper said with a smile. "Who is it, Frank or Jesse?"

That night Clint said good-bye to Nancy Colvin, a young lady he'd been seeing while he was in Denver. The good-bye took place in his room, and took quite some time.

Nancy had a long, lean body but large breasts, and Clint took his time saying good-bye to every inch of her with his hands and his mouth. He was nestled between her legs, his face buried in her bush, his tongue avid, tasting her, licking her until she put both of her hands on his head and said, "God, stop! You're gonna kill me. Come up here and put yourself inside me."

He obliged, lying atop her, lifting his hips and then sliding into her. He slid in so easily because she was all wet from his earlier attentions with his tongue.

She wrapped her legs around him, placing her heels on his buttocks, and he moved in and out of her. She licked his shoulder and his neck, then bit him as she felt her climax building. He slid his hands beneath her, cupping her taut buttocks, pulling her closer to him, burying himself deeper and deeper until, finally, she seemed to erupt beneath him, bucking and writhing and then moaning out loud when he exploded inside of her. . . .

"Do you have to leave?" she asked later.

"Yes."

"Why?" She nestled close to him, her head on his shoulder, her hand on his thigh.

"I've been invited to a wedding."

"Is it a good friend who's getting married?"

"Well . . . not exactly, but I owe it to him to be there."

"Will you be coming back to Denver?"

"I'm sure I will," he said. "It's one of my favorite cities."

"It was one of mine, too," she said, "but starting tomorrow it won't be."

"Why not?"

"Because you won't be in it."

"I'm sure there are plenty of young men in Denver who will want to help you forget me, Nancy."

"Well, it won't work," she said, "but I guess there's no harm in letting them try."

TWELVE

Clint got to Kearney, Missouri, the day before the wedding. He couldn't ride out to Jesse's mother's house for two reasons. One, he didn't know where it was, and two, he might have gotten shot. So he checked into the hotel and waited for the James boys to get word to him.

He was sitting in the saloon with a beer, wondering how Jesse knew to send the telegram to Denver, when a man entered, spotted him, and walked over to his table.

"You Adams?"

"That's right."

"Name's Morrow, Ben Morrow," the man said. "Shake my hand like we're old friends."

Clint stood up and the two men shook with feigned warmth.

"Now get me a beer."

Clint thought the man might be pushing it, but he went along with him.

When he returned with the beer the man said, "I'm supposed to give you directions to the house."

"Whose house?"

"Whose do you think?" the man asked.

"Jesse's ma?"

"No, they're gettin' hitched at Zee's sister's house. Her name's Brander."

"Oh."

"You can't write these directions down."

"I think I'll be able to remember," Clint said.

The man gave him the directions, which were brief and easy to remember.

"You got them?" Morrow asked.

"I've got them."

"You want me to repeat them?"

"No."

"Suit yourself," Morrow said. He drank down half the beer and stood up. "Oh, if you didn't already buy a wedding present, don't. Not in town, anyway."

"Is there anyplace else?"

"Not for miles."

"You want to shake hands again before you leave?" Clint asked.

"Naw," the man said. "See you at the wedding."

With that Morrow left, and Clint wondered if the man was a relative or just a friend to the James family.

Clint nursed his beer, since he had most of the day and night to kill until morning, when the wedding was scheduled. He was still drinking his beer when another man walked in, saw him, and came walking over. This one was wearing a badge.

"Are you Clint Adams?"

"That's right," Clint said. "You want to shake hands?"

"What fer?" the man asked.

"I don't know," Clint said. "What do you want?"

"I was just wondering what brought you to Kearney, Adams."

"Any special reason why you're asking, Sheriff?"

"Because it's my job."

"How'd you know I was here?"

"Somebody recognized you, came and told me."

"Why don't you have a seat."

"Don't want to sit with you, Adams," the sheriff said, "just wanted to ask you a question."

Clint studied the sheriff, a tall, well-built man in his early thirties who seemed unimpressed with him.

"I'm just passing through, Sheriff."

"How long you plan on stayin'?"

"Probably just two nights."

"Not lookin' for trouble, are you?"

"I'm never looking for it, Sheriff."

"Always seems to find men like you, though, don't it?" the sheriff asked.

"Does it?"

"Just be warned," the sheriff said. "I won't hold with no gunplay in my town."

"I'm not looking for any gunplay, Sheriff—I know," he said then, holding his hand up, "it always finds men like me, don't it?"

"Just remember what I said, Adams," the man said and stalked out.

Clint finished his beer and decided he had better leave the saloon before somebody else came looking for him.

THIRTEEN

The next morning Clint reclaimed his horse from the livery and followed the directions he'd been given to get to the wedding. When he got to the end of the directions he realized he was in a clearing in the middle of nowhere. He settled down to wait. Soon he heard a horse approaching, and then saw a horse and rider and smiled.

"You follow directions real good, ol' hoss," Frank James said.

Frank rode up to him and the two shook hands. Clint noticed that Frank seemed to have aged five years in the year since they'd last seen each other. The outlaw life was a hard one.

"You ready to go to a weddin'?" Frank asked.

"As long as it isn't mine."

"Amen to that," Frank said. "Come on. Follow me."

When they reached the house Clint was surprised to see how many people were there. He'd thought this would be a small, private affair, to keep from attracting too much attention. Apparently, he was the only one who thought that would have been the prudent thing to do.

"Dingus don't do things in a small way," Frank said.

"I can see that."

"Come on, I'll introduce you to Ma."

They dismounted and someone appeared to take their horses. Clint realized it was Ben Morrow.

"Howdy," Morrow said, and walked the animals off.

Clint could smell food cooking, but no one was eating yet.

Along the way Clint met other family members, including Jesse and Frank's uncle, the Reverend William James, who would be performing the wedding ceremony. He also met Zee's sister and her husband, who had lent their home to the event. On more than one occasion Frank introduced Clint as the man who had saved his life twice. This endeared Clint to each person he met.

Finally, they found Frank and Jesse's mother, who grabbed him and hugged him tightly upon introduction.

"Mr. Adams, I can't thank you enough for what you done for my boys," she said. "I'm pleased you were able to come to the wedding."

"I'm glad to be here, Mrs. Samuels," he said. He'd been introduced to her by her present married name.

"And here's the groom," Frank said.

Clint turned and saw Jesse walking toward them, tall and handsome in a fine black broadcloth suit and colorful vest and tie.

"Clint!" Jesse said and pumped his hand happily. "Real glad you could make it."

"I didn't know I had a choice," Clint said so only Jesse could hear him.

"Sure you had a choice," Jesse said, clapping him on the shoulder, "and you made the right one. I'd introduce you to my beautiful bride, but I ain't supposed to see her before the ceremony. Superstition."

"So I've heard."

"Have you met everybody?"

"I met your uncle, your future sister-in-law, and your mother, as well as other family members."

"Then Frank's been a good host," Jesse said. Clint was surprised that while Frank looked older and tired, Jesse was beaming, and looking younger. Of course, that could have had something to do with the fact that this was his wedding day.

"You know something?" Jesse asked, rubbing his hands together.

"What?"

"I'm more nervous today than any time we robbed a train, or a bank, or had a posse on our heels. Ain't that silly?"

"Probably not," Clint said. "You were familiar with those things. This is something totally new."

"You know, you're right," Jesse said. "I guess I ain't bein' so silly."

"Jess," Frank said. "They're ready for you."

"Talk to you after the weddin'," Jesse said to Clint. "Thanks again for comin'."

"Sure, Jesse," Clint said, wishing he'd had a chance to talk to Jesse about Denver. Obviously, that would have to wait until later.

FOURTEEN

The wedding was a grand thing, so well attended that Clint wondered if there was anyone left in town. Jesse looked very handsome, indeed, and his new young wife, Zee, was lovely. His uncle William performed the ceremony proudly and well, and when he announced, "You may kiss the bride," the hooting and hollering started but did not deter Jesse from kissing his new bride soundly.

And then the food was served.

There was steak, and ribs, and corn, and all kinds of other vegetables, and Clint ate his fill while fielding questions from both sides of Jesse's family. At one point, as Clint was walking about with a plate of food, looking for a place to sit and eat, he came face-to-face with another man in the same predicament—and was surprised to find that it was the sheriff. The man simply nodded to him, smiled, and moved on.

After he had finished eating, Clint went to get himself a glass of punch from one of several huge bowls. He heard his name called from behind. He turned and saw Jesse approaching, with Zee in tow.

"Clint Adams," he said proudly, "meet Zerelda James, my wife."

Zee held out her hand and smiled, a dazzling smile that warmed Clint with its glow.

"Jesse's told me so much about you, Mr. Adams . . ."

"Please, call me Clint."

"And you must call me Zee. We are so grateful for everything you did for Jesse and Frank last year, around Hermann. You are a great hero to our family."

"Am I?"

"Oh, indeed you are, Clint. Please don't be so modest about it."

"Clint's a very modest man," Jesse said. "He just can't help it."

"Well, I expect to see a lot of you, Clint. When Jesse and I are settled in our own home you must come and visit."

"I will, Zee."

She took both his hands and said, "Promise?"

"I promise."

"And now I must go and inquire as to whether our guests need anything else. You'll excuse me?"

"Of course."

Zee kissed Jesse and was swallowed up by the crowd.

"Jesse," Clint said, "I saw the sheriff here."

"He's anywhere he can get free food," Jesse said. "Don't worry, Clint. These are all my family, my friends, my neighbors. Frank and I, we're safe here."

"Jesse, can we talk?"

"About what?"

"Denver."

"Ah."

"How did you know I was there?"

"I didn't," Jesse said.

"But you sent a telegram—"

"I sent many telegrams, hoping one of them would find you," Jesse said, cutting him off. "I guess the one I sent to Denver did, huh?"

"Obviously."

Could it be, then, that Jesse didn't know that Clint had been working for the Pinkertons last year, when they met?

"I've got something to show you," Jesse said. "Come with me."

Despite the fact that it was Jesse's wedding day, the man was still wearing his guns. Clint remembered something Frank had said last year, in Hermann. He said he'd never seen anyone shoot like Clint, except Jesse. Clint hoped that Jesse never got the desire to prove who was better.

He followed the outlaw to the barn.

"Lots of weddin' presents inside," Jesse said. "Why do farmers give livestock as wedding presents?"

"They figure what's precious to them will be precious to others, I guess," Clint said.

"I suppose you're right. Come inside."

Clint followed Jesse into the barn.

"Horses," Jesse said. "We got six of 'em."

"They look fine."

"What do you think of this one?"

Jesse walked to the last stall to show Clint the horse standing in it. When Clint saw the animal he was brought up short. It was huge, and black as night, and in its eyes was a look of intelligence he had never seen before in a horse.

"He's magnificent," Clint said. "What is he, three?"

"Just turned three, and gelded. He'll keep his mind on business."

Clint couldn't help but approach the animal, who bobbed his massive head up and down before succumbing to Clint's touch.

"Easy, big boy, easy, big fella," he said, patting the gelding's neck. "Jesse, whoever gave you this animal sure knows his horses. I've never seen anything like him."

"He wasn't given to me," Jesse said.

"What?"

"He's yours."

"What?" Clint was amazed. "What do you mean?"

"This horse is my family's way of saying thank you for what you did for Frank last year. You risked your life—

twice—and lost your horse. I see you've replaced him. Are you attached to the one you have now?"

"No," Clint admitted, "I've had several since then, but I can't find one I'm satisfied with."

"Think you'd be satisfied with this one?"

"Of course I would," Clint said, "but, Jesse, I can't accept a gift like this."

"It took me a year to find a horse I thought would suit you," Jesse said. "I finally did, and now that I've given him to you, you can't insult me and my family by turning our gift down."

"I don't want to insult anyone, Jesse—"

"Good, then it's settled," Jesse said. "He's yours."

Clint looked the horse over again, still amazed at such a gift.

"What's his name?" he asked.

"That's up to you."

"He's regal-looking," Clint said, "like some kind of royalty."

"King?" Jesse suggested.

"That doesn't suit him."

"Prince, then."

Clint hesitated, then said, "No, not that, either."

"What then?"

Clint thought a moment longer then said, "Duke," and the horse lifted his head, as if reacting to the name. "You like that, Duke?" Clint asked the horse. "You want that for a name?"

The horse seemed to nod his head, although Clint knew it couldn't be possible.

"I guess that's it, then," Clint said, turning to his host. "Jesse, meet Duke."

FIFTEEN

APRIL 5, 1882

Clint rose early on the morning they were supposed to pick up Jesse's body and take it to the railroad station. He went down to the lobby of his hotel where he found Ben Morrow and Sim Whitsett.

"You boys are early."

"Can't be too early," Ben Morrow said.

"Had breakfast?"

"Nope."

"Come on," Clint said, "I'll buy," and he led them into the hotel dining room.

Over breakfast Ben Morrow suddenly said, "I got a confession to make."

"About what, Ben?" Whitsett asked.

"Not to you, ya durn fool," Morrow said, and then looked at Clint. "To you."

"To me? What for, Ben?"

"Somethin' that happened eight years ago," Morrow said, "the day of Jesse's weddin' to Zee."

"Eight years is a long time, Ben," Clint said. "Why don't you just keep it to yourself and I'll say no hard feelings."

"Naw," Morrow said, "I got to get this out."

"All right, then," Clint said, giving the man his full attention, "go ahead."

"The day Jesse got married," Morrow said, "it was me told the sheriff you was in town."

"Ben," Clint said, "the sheriff was at Jesse's wedding. He would have seen me there, anyway."

Morrow looked surprised.

"Oh, yeah . . . but still, I was kind of jealous of you back then, you know, 'cause Jesse and Frank respected you so much."

"That's okay, Ben," Clint said. "Like I said, that was a long time ago, and there's no hard feelings."

"Well," Morrow said, "at least I got that off my chest."

"Yes, you did."

The body was turned over to Sheriff Timberlake, who in turn gave it over to the James women, Jesse's mother and wife. Clint was there, while Ben Morrow and Sim Whitsett were already at the train station. That was where Clint thought trouble would come, if it came at all.

They placed Jesse's body on a buckboard, and then both his mother and wife climbed onto the seat. Clint rode alongside on Duke, which he thought was fitting, Jesse being the one who had presented the big gelding to him on the day of his wedding.

A crowd walked along with the buckboard, but Clint didn't feel there was any danger from them. Most of them were mourning Jesse, some of the women crying and reaching up to hold the hand of Jesse's mother or wife.

At the train station Jesse's casket was taken off the buckboard by Clint, Ben, Sim, and Sheriff Timberlake. The two women followed behind them. As they approached the baggage car of the train, where the casket would be riding, there was a shot. Clint and the other men immediately put the casket down and turned. Jesse's mother was on the ground, having been pulled down by Zee, who was on top of her mother-in-law, covering her with her own body.

"Clint, somebody shot at Ma."

Clint's gun was out, as were Ben Morrow's and Sim Whitsett's.

"Put up your guns, boys," the sheriff said, scanning the crowd. "Whoever did it is gone. It was probably just a prank, and not a serious attempt to kill Mrs. Samuels."

Clint thought the sheriff was probably right.

"Let's get this casket on board," Timberlake said.

They holstered their guns and carried Jesse's casket onto the baggage car.

"That's it," the sheriff said. "I'm done with this."

Before Clint could say anything, the man got off the train and walked away.

"Ben, you and Sim ride with the casket, okay?"

"Sure," Morrow said.

"Where we goin'?" Whitsett asked.

"Kearney," Clint said. "I'll give you fare to come back."

"That don't matter," Morrow said. "You just go and see to Jesse's women."

"I'll see you boys in Kearney."

Clint stepped down from the baggage car, and the door was closed behind him. There were no further incidents as he walked Jesse's mother and wife onto the train and got them seated. Soon, the train was moving and they were leaving St. Joseph, Missouri, behind.

SIXTEEN

On the train was a marshal named Craig, who was there to see that the body made it safely to its destination.

They had taken the train to Cameron, Missouri, where they were supposed to switch to a special train that would take them to Kearney. Now that Jesse was dead, the law was being very cooperative with the family in getting his body home for burial. Still, the special train never arrived, and Marshal Craig had the body moved from the baggage car of the train to the caboose of a freight train. Clint helped the James women onto the freight train, and this was what they took to Kearney.

It was an all-night trip and they arrived in Kearney early on April 6. As Jesse's mother and Zee got off the train with Clint they were met by other family members, specifically Jesse's cousin, L. W. James, and Zee's brother, R. T. Mimms. Jesse's body was removed from the train and taken to the Kearney Hotel, where it was put on public display. It would remain there for people to see until two p.m., when it would be moved to the Mt. Olivet Baptist Church for a funeral ceremony. Before being moved, however, it was placed in a different casket, a metal vault of imitation rosewood that was engraved with the name "Jesse James."

The hearse was followed by hundreds of people, none of

whom were allowed inside the church. Only the family was allowed, and Clint—for all intents and purposes—was considered family. He sat with Mrs. Samuels and Zee.

The pastor of the church, one J. M. P. Martin, officiated at the service, assisted by a Reverend R. H. Jones of Lathrop, Missouri.

People had turned out for this funeral from all over Missouri, and they fairly surrounded the church while the service was being said inside.

After the service the body was again put on the wagon and was taken to the site of Jesse's early home, where he would be buried.

Jesse's half brother, John Samuels, had been injured in a brawl at a dance hall and was unable to attend the funeral. He was in the house, though, and was allowed to take one last look at Jesse. Clint heard later that some people thought Frank was in the house, too. He didn't see Frank there, though.

Finally, Jesse's body was buried in a deep grave in the yard by the kitchen. Jesse's mother, however, suddenly became hysterical and claimed that someone had cut off her son's right hand. So adamant was she that the casket had to be raised up again and opened to satisfy her that her son was intact. She calmed down after that, and Jesse was buried.

Zee did not stay in the house next to Jesse's grave. She insisted on staying at the Kearney Hotel until the next day, whereupon she would board the train again and head back to St. Joseph.

"It's my home," she said, as Clint drove her back to Kearney. Duke was following behind the buckboard. "Maybe we weren't living there under our real names, but that's our home, and that is where I will live with my children."

"Is someone trying to talk you out of it, Zee?"

She turned her head and looked at Clint.

"Many people, Clint," she said. "I've had offers for the

house, lots of money, but I won't sell, no matter how badly I might need money."

"There are ways to get money, Zee."

"How?"

"Give up some items to be auctioned."

"Never."

"It doesn't have to be anything that means anything to you," he said. "An old gun, some other effects that you can say were Jesse's."

"That would be dishonest," she said.

He remained silent.

"Those souvenir hunting ghouls would end up with junk."

"Yes," he said, "they would."

She laughed suddenly and put her hand on his arm.

"By God, I'll do it," she said happily. "It will serve them right!"

At the hotel Clint got Zee a room and then saw her to it. They had to fight their way through a sea of people to get into the lobby, though.

At the door to her room Clint said, "Just stay in the room, Zee, until I come for you."

"I'm like a prisoner," she said.

He didn't know what to say to that.

"I'll come and get you later for some dinner."

"Will you come back to St. Joe with me?"

"Yes."

"And you'll still talk to Frank?"

"I will," he said, "but when, and where?"

"Frank will pick the place, and the time. We'll just have to be ready."

"All right," he said. "I'll be ready."

"Thank you, Clint, for everything."

He waited until she went inside and closed the door, and as he walked away down the hall he thought he could hear crying from inside the room.

SEVENTEEN

Clint was once again thinking back to the day Jesse got married when there was a knock at his hotel room door. He answered the door with his gun in his hand, and lowered the gun when he saw that his caller was Zee James.

"Zee," he said, stepping back. "Is everything all right?"

"Can I come in?" she asked, looking up and down the hall. "Before someone sees me?"

"Of course."

She stepped into the room and Clint closed the door. He turned and realized she was wearing a robe over a nightgown. Luckily, no one *had* seen her.

He walked to the bedpost and holstered his gun.

"I can't sleep," she said. "My mind is whirling with memories."

"So is mine," he said. "In fact, when you knocked I was thinking back to your wedding day, when Jesse gave me Duke."

She smiled.

"He was so excited to give you that horse, and so proud over the years when he heard you still had him. Can I sit?"

"Of course."

She sat on the bed as he stood awkwardly by. Zee James was a very attractive woman, with hair like corn and pale skin, but she was his friend's wife—widow. Having her in his room made him nervous.

She stared down at her hands, which were intertwined in her lap.

"I don't know what to do. I can't sleep, and lying awake is no good either." She looked up at him with her blue eyes. "I thought maybe we could talk."

"We can talk all night, if you want, Zee."

"That wouldn't be fair to you," she said. "You've got to get some sleep."

"Oh, that's okay—"

"Do you know what Jesse would do when I couldn't sleep?"

"What?"

"He'd just hold me."

Clint didn't say anything. He could see that Zee was as nervous as he was.

"Clint?"

"Yes?"

"Could you?"

"Could I what?"

"Hold me," she said. She looked down, then back at him, boldly. "Could I just . . . sleep with you, with your arms around me?"

"Zee—"

"I'm not looking for anything else," she said hurriedly, "and I'm not offering anything. I just . . . don't want to be alone tonight."

He studied her for a few moments, then decided he was being silly. A man and a woman could lie in the same bed together without sex becoming an issue. After all, she made it clear she wasn't offering herself to him. She just needed some help, tonight.

"Sure, Zee," he said. "I'd be . . . happy to."

She stood up and he pulled down the bedclothes. She removed her robe and got into bed clad only in her cotton nightgown. For a moment Clint wondered what to do about his clothes. He had removed his boots, but was still wearing his Levi's and shirt.

"I—I could go back to my room, if this is too awkward," she offered.

"It's awkward, Zee," he said. "I won't lie to you, but just give me a minute and I'll be able to deal with it."

"You can come to bed . . . in your underwear. That's all right. I'm really . . . not after your body."

"I know that," he said, and suddenly he saw that she was amused by his dilemma.

He decided to brazen it out. He removed his shirt, then his pants, and got into bed with her. He pulled the sheets up over them.

"I usually lie like this," she said, rolling onto her right side.

"Okay." He moved over and did the same, pressing himself against her, sliding one arm over her. She nestled herself back against him, and when her bottom pressed on him he reacted the way any man would have.

"Oh . . ." she said, feeling his hardness against her.

"Sorry," he said, "I don't have any control over that."

"It's . . . all right."

He tried to get comfortable and his hand accidently closed over her right breast just long enough for him to feel her hard nipple.

"Sorry," he said.

She giggled and said, "I don't have any control over that either."

"Zee . . ."

"Oh, it's all right, Clint," she said soothingly. "We're friends, and you're just helping me to sleep. Jesse wouldn't think anything of it."

"He wouldn't?"

"No," she said, and abruptly she turned over to face him. "We're just two people trying to help each other through a rough time . . . a rough night."

Her face was very close to his, and she was so pretty. He

could feel her sweet breath on his face. She put her arm over him and pressed herself to him. He could feel the hardness of her nipples through her nightgown on his bare chest. He put his arms around her and held her that way, his hardness trapped between them, nestled against her belly.

"Zee," he said, "this might not be such a good idea."

She didn't answer.

"Zee," he said, "I don't think . . ."

He trailed off when he realized that she had fallen asleep. Somehow, though, that didn't make it much easier for him.

EIGHTEEN

When Clint woke the next day he was on his back and Zee was lying on his shoulder. His arm was around her, and it took a moment for him to realize that her nightgown had hiked up around her waist and his hand had been resting on her bare buttock. He left it there for a moment, afraid that snatching it away might wake her. He moved his hand, though, and suddenly his middle finger found the crease between her buttocks. She moaned in her sleep and moved her butt, slid her hand over his chest. Suddenly, he felt her lips on his bare chest and her hand slid down between them. Sure that she was still asleep he dared not wake her. She slipped her hand into his underwear and began to stroke his erect penis. He gritted his teeth because it felt so good. She closed her hand around him and held him gently, then slid her hand lower so she could caress his balls. He began to knead her buttocks, which were smooth and firm, and her mouth was avid on his chest. Suddenly, he knew she was awake as she slid one leg over him. She pushed his underwear down far enough so she could mount him and take him inside. She was incredibly wet and hot, and he slid in all the way, and then she began to move. She was lying flat on him, so he couldn't see her face, which was nestled against the side of his neck. He held her buttocks and moved with her, and she started to moan and move more quickly. Apparently she was very ready right from the start because her climax came quickly. She whimpered and bit his shoulder, and he felt something hot on his skin. It took him a moment to realize that it was tears.

She continued to move on him until he grunted and exploded inside of her. She slid off of him then, but remained pressed against him, her head on his shoulder, and he realized that she wanted to pretend that she was still asleep. That was probably the smart way to handle this, he thought, so he went along with it. It took a few moments, but they both eventually relaxed, and then they both fell into a deep sleep.

The second time they awoke they pretended it was the first.

"Mmm," she said, stretching and rolling away from him. "Good morning."

"Good morning."

She pulled her nightgown down so it covered her hips and crotch, and he kept his eyes averted until she'd done so. He adjusted his own underwear so that he was adequately covered.

"How did you sleep?" he asked.

"Like a log," she said. "I never thought I'd sleep that well again. Thank you for letting me stay with you last night."

"You're welcome. Are you hungry?"

"Famished," she said. "That's a surprise, too."

"Why don't we get dressed and have some breakfast, and then you can tell me what you want to do before you head back to St. Joe."

"That's fine," she said, sitting up. "I'll go to my room, get dressed, and meet you in the lobby. Shall we eat right in the hotel?"

"I think that would be wise."

"All right, then."

She stood up and her nightgown fell down the rest of the way to cover her. She walked to the door, put her hand on the doorknob, then turned to look at him. Was she going to bring it up?

"Clint?"

"Yes?"

She looked at him, bit her lip, then shook her head and said, "Nothing. I'll see you downstairs in half an hour."

"All right."

She left, looking both ways and then closing the door gently behind her. He put his hands behind his head and stared at the ceiling, trying to decide how he felt. Guilty? Ashamed? Disappointed, because he hadn't been able to give in to the urge to have her fully, to explore her lovely body with his hands and his mouth, to enjoy the way she felt and smelled?

He looked down at himself and realized he was erect again. Zee James was a lovely woman and under any other circumstances he probably would have tried to keep her in bed with him all day.

He decided that he didn't have anything to feel guilty about. He had not forced himself on her. True, he hadn't pushed her away, but she apparently needed what she had gotten from him, and if she wanted to handle it by pretending she was asleep through it, and ignoring it, that was fine with him. After all, he'd been willing to give her what she needed last night, so why stop now?

He got up and walked to the window, looked down at the main street. Nobody was out there. He thought there might be a crowd of people gathered in front of the hotel, and was pleased that there wasn't. Maybe they'd leave Zee alone today.

He was about to leave the window when he spotted a man in a doorway across the street, watching the hotel. He was wearing a brown vested suit and a bowler hat, looking distinctly out of place in Kearney, Missouri. The man would have fit in much better in Denver, where Clint knew he was from.

His name was Carl Burns, and he was a Pinkerton.

NINETEEN

Clint got down to the lobby before Zee and left the hotel. He went directly across the street, and when Burns saw him coming he wasn't sure how to react. He tried to go into the store whose doorway he was standing in, but it wasn't open yet and the door was locked. Then he tried to step out of the doorway, but Clint was there by then and pushed him back in. Burns was not an imposing figure. He carried a lot of weight, most of it in his belly.

"Hello, Carl."

"Oh, uh, hello, Adams. What are you doing here?"

"You know why I'm here, Carl," Clint said, "and I know why you're here—that is, unless Allan Pinkerton got wise and fired you."

"No, I ain't fired," Burns said. "I still work for the Pinkertons."

"And he sent you here to check up on Jesse's funeral, right? To make sure he was dead?"

"So? I'm just here doing my job."

"And when you sent Pinkerton a telegram and told him I was here? What was his reaction?"

"I, uh, don't know what you—"

"Sure you do, Carl. He probably said that he knew all along that I was in with the James boys, and he wanted you to keep an eye on me and see what I was doing here."

"I, uh—"

"So you followed me here to Kearney, and to the hotel. I'm surprised I didn't spot you, Carl."

"It's my job to follow people—"

"I'll bet it was an accident," Clint said, cutting him off.

"Huh?"

"I'll bet you didn't follow me at all. You knew they were bringing Jesse here to bury him, so you came ahead, and when you saw me, it was an accident."

Burns averted his eyes, and Clint knew he was right. Burns was incompetent, and Clint had often wondered why old Allan kept him employed.

"So what now, Carl? The funeral's over and I'll be leaving town today. What are you going to do?"

"Uh, I don't know—"

"Of course you don't, you haven't heard from Allan and you sure couldn't make a big decision like that yourself, could you?"

"I, uh, gotta go, Adams—" the portly man said, again trying to step from the doorway. Clint put his hand against the man's chest and pushed him back.

"Adams, whataya wanna do that for—"

"Give Allan a message for me, Carl."

"Uh, sure, what message?"

"Tell him to leave the James family alone. Tell him it's over. Jesse's dead, and without Jesse there is no James gang. I want him to leave Jesse's mother, and wife, alone. Understand?"

"Sure, but what about Frank?"

"Frank's not going to form another gang, not without Jesse. Tell Allan what I said. It's all over."

"Uh, yeah, sure."

"Now get out of here."

Clint stepped back and allowed the man to step out of the doorway and scurry away. He watched Burns until he turned a corner, then walked back across the street to the hotel. As he entered the lobby Zee was coming down the steps.

"Where did you go?"

"Just to talk to somebody," he said. "Come on, let's eat."

As they went into the dining room she asked, "Who were you talking to?"

"Let's sit down first."

When they were seated and had ordered coffee, he told Zee about Carl Burns.

"Those Pinkertons!" she spat. "They won't leave us alone. Isn't it enough they almost killed us once?"

"I sent Allan a message, Zee," Clint said. "I told him to leave you alone, that there was no James gang without Jesse. Was I right?"

"How would I know?"

"You'd know. Will Frank try to put together another James gang?"

"There never was a James gang, Clint," she said. "There was always the James-Younger gang, and after Northfield that was over. You know that."

"Yes," he said, "I do know that."

"So the answer is, no, Frank will not try to put together a James gang. What he might do, however, is try to kill Bob Ford."

"Where is Frank, Zee? Do you know?"

"No."

"Was he at the house? I thought I heard someone say he was inside."

She hesitated.

"You asked me to talk to him, Zee," he said. "I can't do that if I don't know where he is."

"He was inside," she said. "He said he had to come to Jesse's funeral."

"I can't say I blame him for that. Can you arrange for me to talk to him?"

"Yes."

"Here, or in St. Joe?"

"St. Joe."

"All right—" Clint said, then stopped short when the waiter appeared with their food. "All right, arrange it for when we get back."

"A-all right."

"When do you want to go back?"

"This afternoon," she said. "I have to get back to my children, but first I have to say good-bye to Ma."

"All right," he said. "I'll take you out to the house, purchase the train tickets, and then come back to get you. That should be enough time for you to arrange things with Frank."

"I won't see Frank, but I'll have Ma arrange it."

"That's fine. Now let's eat, and then we'll go out to the house."

She started to eat, then stopped and asked, "Do you think they will, Clint?"

"Who will?"

"The Pinkertons," she said. "Do you think they'll leave us alone?"

"I hope so, Zee," he said. "I really hope so."

TWENTY

One year after Jesse James's wedding

It was a full year after Jesse's wedding that the infamous "bombing" took place.

When he heard about Jesse's wedding, and what a public thing it was, Allan Pinkerton grew livid. He had sent an agent named John Whicher into Missouri to track Jesse, and the man had shown up dead shortly thereafter. Pinkerton couldn't prove it, but he felt sure that Jesse James had killed his man.

Pinkerton knew what the situation was in Missouri. He knew that Jesse's luck depended on the help he received from the people of Missouri, especially his neighbors in Clay County, so he came up with a plan. He had to convince these people that Frank and Jesse James were nothing but common criminals. He launched a campaign that took almost a year, but toward the end of that time people were starting to believe that the James boys had stretched the sympathy from the Civil War a bit too far.

So it was a year after Jesse's wedding that Pinkerton heard that Frank and Jesse would be at the home of their mother, the James-Samuels farm.

William Pinkerton, Allan's brother, arrived in Kansas City

to head up the operation. He would coordinate the effort with all of the information he received from spies on "Castle James," as he had started to call it. From Kansas City he went to the town of Liberty, in Clay County, and began to gather his forces. When the word came that Frank and Jesse had actually been seen at the home of their mother, Pinkerton sent for his men, and a detachment of Pinkerton agents arrived on the train from Kansas City. Locals met them at the station and led them to a locale near the James-Samuels farm, where Pinkerton was waiting.

Late that night these men placed themselves at strategic points near the farm, and waited for their orders.

Clint found himself in the vicinity of Kearney, Missouri, around that time and decided to stop in and see Jesse's mother, a woman he had become rather fond of. When he arrived at her home he was greeted warmly by her and her husband, Dr. Samuels. They fed him, and demanded that he stay the night with them. He agreed, and thus became a part of this chapter of the story of the Pinkertons' constant attempts to catch Frank and Jesse James.

When William Pinkerton gave the word, two men approached the James farmhouse carrying turpentine balls, meant to light the house. When they attempted to open the shutters on one of the windows, they awoke an old black servant, who sounded the alarm.

Inside the house Clint heard the servant shouting and went to the window of the room he was in. He didn't see anyone, but he did see the glow of a turpentine ball. He knew what they were used for, and knew that something was amiss. A plan was being put into effect, here, and he knew the potential danger to the people in the house.

He ran from his room to the Samuelses' room and woke Jesse's mother and her husband.

"We have to get out of the house," he said urgently.

"There are children in the house," Mrs. Samuels said. "Let's get them and get out."

"What's going on?" Dr. Samuels asked, struggling into his pants.

"There's someone outside, some—"

It was at that point someone from outside threw a turpentine ball into the house, shattering a window.

They all ran downstairs and saw that the kitchen was on fire.

"Get everyone out!" Clint shouted.

Something else came through the window, and Clint saw another turpentine ball rolling across the floor. Dr. Samuels reacted immediately and tried to kick it into the fireplace. Abruptly, he grabbed a broom and used it to get the ball into the fireplace, onto the hot coals.

"No!" Clint shouted, but it was too late.

Like a bomb, the thing exploded.

TWENTY-ONE

Pieces of the turpentine ball flew from the fireplace. One struck Mrs. Samuels on the arm, cutting her badly. Dr. Samuels was stunned. Later, the incident would be described in several newspapers as a bombing. The Pinkertons would deny they had any bombs with them.

Clint grabbed the injured woman and shouted for the others to get out of the house. He dragged her from the house and away from it before lying her down on the ground to see how badly she was wounded. He tore some pieces from his shirt to bandage her temporarily then turned and looked at the Pinkertons, many of whom were also startled by what had happened.

"Which one of you sons of bitches threw those balls into the house?"

In reply several shots were fired at the house, but immediately thereafter the Pinkertons began to retreat. It was obvious to them that Frank and Jesse had not been inside and that they had burned Dr. Samuels, women, and children out of the house—clearly not the intention of Allan or William Pinkerton.

Dr. Samuels staggered over to where his wife lay injured and tended to her wound, which was between the elbow and hand. Later, her arm would have to be amputated.

Clint stood and watched the Pinkertons flee. He was tempted to shoot some of them, but what would that accomplish, except maybe to make him as sought after by their boss as Frank and Jesse were. There had only been one man in the attacking force he thought he'd recognized, and that was William Pinkerton. It figured that Allan would send his brother to head up this disaster. Clint only hoped that his friend Talbot Roper had done as he'd planned and left the Pinkertons before this had occurred. He hated to think that Roper might have taken part in this fiasco.

"What happened?" he heard Mrs. Samuels say. "Who were they?"

"Hush, dear," Dr. Samuels replied, but she was adamant.

"Who were they, Clint?" she demanded. "Who were those men who burned down my house?!"

"They were Pinkertons," Clint said, as both Dr. Samuels and his wife looked up at him. "Pinkertons, looking for Jesse and Frank."

"But they're not here," she said. "My boys aren't here."

"I know that, Ma," Clint said, "I know that."

"Clint?"

He looked across the table at Zee, who had startled him from his reverie and brought him back to the present. She was staring at him, her lovely face etched with concern.

"Are you all right?"

"I'm fine," he said, "fine, Zee. I was just . . . thinking back."

"I've been doing a lot of that lately. It's hard to believe Jesse's been dead three days."

"I know," Clint said. "It seems much longer."

"I've finished eating," she said. "Shall we go? I want to see Ma, make sure she's all right."

"Yes," Clint said, "yes, let's go."

She hesitated before getting up, and for a moment he thought she might approach what had happened between them that morning. Instead, she simply rose and started to walk out ahead of him. He breathed a sigh of relief, because he would not have known what to say to her. If she felt guilt, he would not have known how to soothe her, and if she had suddenly become accusatory, he would not have known how to defend himself.

It was better this way, he thought as he followed her out. Just let it be.

TWENTY-TWO

On the train back to St. Joe they talked about the rift between Jesse and Frank.

"They had stopped thinking alike," Zee said. "I think that was the problem. Only they knew for sure what was wrong."

"And how bad was it?"

"They were apart," she said. "How often do you know of that happening?"

"Not often."

"And yet when Jesse would plan something and call for Frank, he'd come, no questions asked."

"Well . . . they were brothers. Frank once explained the importance of that to me—and, even more, the importance of being the older brother."

They rode in silence for a while and then she said, "It was Northfield."

He looked at her.

"That's when it started," she said, looking at him, "Northfield, and you were there."

"Yes, I was."

"Jesse never told me what happened, Clint."

He knew what was coming, and wished to head it off.

"Zee—"

"You have to tell me," she said. "That's when it all started going bad."

"Zee, if Jesse didn't tell you—"

"What does it matter, Clint?" she asked. "Jesse's dead."

"Frank's not."

"You need Frank's permission?"

"No, that's not it."

"Then what?"

"I just don't feel it's my place—"

"Then whose is it? Frank's? He won't tell me anything. Clint, I have a right to know what made the last six years so hard."

He was amazed that she only thought of the last six years as hard. What about her whole life with Jesse, being married to him while he was the most hunted man in the country? Why wasn't that hard?

"Clint," she said, taking hold of his arm, "what happened in Northfield?"

"All right, Zee," he said, "I'll tell you. . . ."

TWENTY-THREE

NORTHFIELD, MINNESOTA, 1876

To Clint one of the amazing things about his relationship with the James boys was how he crossed paths with them at what seemed to be crossroads times of their lives. For a man who hated coincidence, Clint accepted this readily. He felt that Jesse—and Frank, as well—were special people, the kind of people who made their own luck. He never held it against them that they chose thievery as a way of life. He knew they felt it was thrust upon them, and he never judged them for it.

He also knew that Jesse had committed murder more than once. Pinkerton, he felt, was right. Jesse had more than likely killed his man, Whicher. Oddly, he never held that against Jesse either. After all, Hickok had killed men and not all of them face-to-face, and Clint considered him to have been his best friend.

And you didn't judge your friends.

Northfield had been the last time Clint had seen Frank and Jesse, until he rode into St. Joe the day Jesse was killed. . . .

Robbing the bank in Northfield, Minnesota, had been the idea of Bill Chadwell. He was a native of that area and knew all the ins and outs. Northfield was a center of farming and cattle, and the bank was extremely wealthy.

The gang, at this point, consisted of Frank and Jesse, Cole, Jim, and Bob Younger, Bill Chadwell, Clell Miller, and Charlie Pitts. They met in a wooded area just outside of Northfield.

Jesse didn't like the idea and wouldn't give it his okay, but Cole Younger had argued for it.

"Chadwell says this bank is rich," Cole said.

"This is a big area for cattle and farming, Jesse," Chadwell said. "This would be our biggest haul ever."

"What's the problem, Jess?" Frank asked. "Why don't you like it?"

"It just don't feel right, Frank," Jesse said. At that point Bob Younger took out a bottle he'd been pulling on. "Put that away!"

"Why should I?" Bob asked and drank again.

"We can't have you bein' drunk, Bob," Jesse said. "You'll get somebody killed."

"Don't you worry," Bob said. "I'll hold up my end. I always do."

"Cole," Jesse said, "you'd better control your brother."

"Don't worry about Bob, Jess," Cole said. "I'll take care of him—but let's do this job. . . ."

The others were all feeling good after the ease with which they had pulled their last robbery, the Rocky Cut Job. So they all agreed with Cole, and Jesse eventually gave in. The clincher was that one of the bank's major stockholders was a Union general, Ben Butler, and this worked on Jesse's sympathies for the Confederacy.

"Well," Jesse said, "if this job will put a hole in that blue belly's pocket . . ."

"It sure as hell will do that," Chadwell assured him.

"Okay, then," Jesse said, still reluctant, "let's do it."

Clint had ridden into Northfield several days earlier and decided to stay awhile. He got himself a room at the Dampier

House Hotel, which was across from the First National Bank, on Scriver Street.

Northfield was split in two, with a wooden bridge connecting the sections, east and west. Clint had found the layout of the town odd, but he also came to learn what a wealthy town it was.

A lot of what he learned he got from a lady named Fay Brannon. Actually, when he rode into Northfield he'd had no intention of doing anything but getting a hot meal, a drink, and a good night's sleep before continuing on. However, he met Fay the first night and, since he had no place in particular to go, decided to stay awhile and enjoy her company.

He woke that morning with Fay wrapped around him. He'd met her in the saloon, but she was not a saloon girl, she was the owner. She had a mass of red hair, the sexiest smile he'd seen in a long time, smooth, tawny skin, and she was young—thirty-two—to be a businesswoman already.

"I'm smart," she had told him the first night, "that's why I'm successful, and that's also why I know a good thing when I see one—and, mister, you're it!"

They'd gone to her room that night and made love in her four-poster, canopy bed that she'd had brought in from Philadelphia. The mattress was the thickest, most comfortable he'd ever been on—for any reason!

On this morning, however, they awoke in his bed, in the hotel. She enjoyed making contact when she slept with a man, and each morning that they had awakened together he'd had to try to disentangle himself from her without waking her. It never happened, which, he suspected, was why she slept that way, to keep him from sneaking away.

"Good morning," she said, with her face pressed into the crook of his neck. Her breath was warm on his neck, and sweet. This was one of the most amazing things he'd noticed about her. She did not appear to have any unpleasant body odors. Most people, when they woke in the morning, had breath that smelled like a bear, but not her. And when she perspired—as she often did, because their sex was frenzied—it never smelled. She was possibly the sweetest woman he'd ever encountered, in taste and smell.

She kissed his neck now, and slid her hand down beneath the sheets. He spread his legs and her hand dipped down so that she touched him lightly with one finger. The sensations brought on by her touch were delicious, and he surrendered himself to them. This was the way to wake up in the morning.

Before long she kissed his chest, then straddled him and kissed his mouth, pushing her tongue into his. He pushed her away so that he could see her breasts, which were full and round with pink nipples that hardened when he just breathed on them. He did not simply breathe now, though, but took them in his mouth, tongued them, sucked them, and bit them until she was squirming atop him.

"You're making me wet," she said, wriggling her butt and sliding her bush over him, wetting his erect penis.

"I can feel it," he said, still holding her breasts, kissing them, "slick and wet and warm . . ."

"Hot," she said, "I'm hot for you."

"What should we do about it?"

"I know what I want to do about it," she whispered. She reached between them, took hold of his rigid penis, held it while she lifted her hips and lowered herself on him.

"Oh, yessss," he said, "definitely a good idea . . ."

TWENTY-FOUR

They slept together and made love together, they even ate dinner together, but never did they eat breakfast or lunch together.

"I don't eat those meals," she had told him that first morning.

"Why not?"

"Those are the meals that make a woman fat."

"You're not fat."

She laughed.

"That's because I don't eat those meals."

So he had taken to eating breakfast alone in the hotel dining room after they dressed and she left to go back to her own place.

Clint ate his breakfast while reading a local newspaper. He read about the Rocky Cut Job, a train that the James-Younger gang had robbed in Otterville, Missouri, at a point in the tracks called Rocky Cut.

"Jesse . . ." he said, shaking his head. While he never judged his friend, he often wished that Frank and Jesse would give up the outlaw life and settle down, but somehow he knew that would never happen. Jesse would end up as Billy the Kid had, and as Bill Hickok had, with a fatal bullet putting an end to his turbulent life.

Somehow, though, he felt that if Jesse were to be killed first, Frank would settle down. He was married now, with children of his own, and Clint had never felt that Frank's commitment to the outlaw life was as strong as Jesse's. But Jesse was the younger brother, and Frank had to look out for him, so Jesse had never pulled a job without Frank.

Clint looked around the dining room and saw faces that had become familiar to him just in the three days he'd been in town. Northfield had impressed him as a well-schooled, law-abiding town like no other. Not only did they have a sheriff and several deputies, but the citizens seemed intent on maintaining law and order. He had witnessed two incidents while he was in town that illustrated this.

His first night in town, in the Northfield Palace, which Fay owned, a fight had broken out over a poker game. As usual, when one man was doing most of the winning, there was always someone who accused him of cheating. Such was the case here. The man making the accusation had stood up abruptly, called the other man a cheater, and gone for his gun. Before the man being accused could react, several men—two from different tables and one from the bar—descended upon the first man and abruptly disarmed him. That done, they took him from the saloon directly to the sheriff's office. Clint had never seen this done as smoothly in any other saloon he'd been in.

"Oh, yes," Fay told him later, when he brought it up, "there's not much crime in Northfield. That's why I like it here."

"Well, that was a bar fight that I saw," Clint said, "or the beginning of one. What about major crimes?"

"Like what? Bank robbery? The last gang that tried to rob the bank got shot to pieces before they could get anywhere. I pity the next gang that tries to rob the First National Bank of Northfield."

The next day he saw a street fight broken up by citizens who had seemingly just been passing by. A store owner also came out of his store to assist, and the two men were hustled off to the sheriff's office.

The sheriff's name was Ken Raiford, and Clint had met him that first day. He was a young man, early thirties, with very dark hair and wide shoulders, who had been sheriff of Northfield for five years. Prior to that he'd been a deputy for three.

"Awful young to have gotten the sheriff's job," Clint had said.

"I learned at the feet of the master," Raiford said. "The sheriff I deputied for was Larry Walker, and he wore that badge here for more than twenty years."

"I've heard of Walker," Clint said. "You did learn from the best. What happened to him?"

"Retired," Walker said. "Left town, left Minnesota. Said he just wanted to get away after all those years of law enforcement around here. Wanted to go someplace where they didn't know him."

"And where did he go?"

"Nobody knows."

Clint had had one or two conversations with the sheriff since then, but brief ones, because the man always seemed to be working.

This morning, however, Raiford was having breakfast in the Dampier House Hotel dining room when Clint entered. The lawman finished eating first, then walked over to Clint's table.

"Mind if I have a cup of coffee with you, Adams?" Raiford asked.

"Sit down, Sheriff," Clint said. "I don't mind at all."

Raiford sat and poured himself a cup.

"To what do I owe this honor?"

"Curiosity."

"About what?"

"You."

Clint waited, then said, "What about me?"

"I was wondering how much longer you were going to be in Northfield."

Clint sat back.

"Can't say I know, exactly," he replied. "Why?"

"Well, you may not have heard this, but folks around here are under the impression that Fay Brannon and I are keeping company."

"Is that a fact?" Clint asked. "Fay didn't mention that."

"Well, that's because she doesn't think so."

"But the town does."

"Yep."

"And you do?"

"Sort of."

"Which means we have a problem with each other?"

"I wouldn't exactly call it a problem," Raiford said. "It's a potential problem, but I guess that depends on how long you figure on staying around."

"Well, I sure don't figure on making it permanent."

"That's good to hear."

"And in fact when I rode in it was originally supposed to be for one night."

"And what happened?"

"Well . . . I met Fay."

Raiford nodded.

"I understand," he said. "She's a fascinating woman."

"Yes, she is. Sheriff, if I had known—"

Raiford held his hand up to stop Clint.

"There's no need for you to say anything," the sheriff said. "I haven't exactly made my feelings known to Fay, but I have to admit, seeing you with her makes me want to."

"So why don't you?"

"I will . . . as soon as you leave town."

"Well," Clint said, "no pressure there. Are you *telling* me to leave town?"

"Not at all," Raiford said. "I just thought we should have a talk. Thanks for the coffee."

The sheriff stood up and walked out of the dining room.

Northfield was the most *civilized* town Clint had ever been to, bar none.

TWENTY-FIVE

Clint stepped out the front door of the Dampier House Hotel and the first person he saw was Bill Chadwell.

He stopped and stared, squinting to make sure he was seeing right. There he was, though, Bill Chadwell standing across the street. The last time Clint had seen Chadwell he was a member of the James-Younger gang. Now Clint had no way of knowing if the man was still affiliated with Frank and Jesse, but there was no reason he could think of that he wouldn't be.

Clint stepped down from the boardwalk and looked up and down the street. He didn't see anyone else he recognized, so he decided to take a turn around town.

Northfield was a busy town and there were people all over the place. It would be easy for a gang to file into town and blend into the scene. What the James-Younger gang didn't know, however—if, indeed, they were in Northfield—was that the people of this town would fight to keep what was theirs. Unlike many other towns Clint had been in—and, indeed, had been a lawman in—this town was not of the opinion that the law should only be upheld by lawmen. If what Fay had told Clint was true, any gang trying to hit the First National Bank here was in for a rude surprise.

• • •

Frank James, Charlie Pitts, and Bob Younger rode into town together, after Bill Chadwell had gone in. While they were waiting to ride in, though, Bob had passed his bottle around and eventually the three men had finished it off. They were certainly not dead drunk when they rode in, but they were feeling no pain.

They rode their horses over the bridge from the west part of town, dismounted and lounged in the square. They were supposed to wait to be joined by Cole Younger and Clell Miller, but the plan went haywire because of the drinking. As soon as Cole and Miller appeared, instead of waiting the first group went into the bank.

It was Jesse!

There was no doubt about it. Jesse James was standing right across the street from him, in front of a café he might just have come out of. Standing next to him was Jim Younger.

Clint crossed the street as calmly as he could, even though he wanted to run and shout at Jesse, "Don't do it! Get out of here!"

He had almost reached them when Jesse turned and saw him coming.

"Well, I'll be damned," Jesse said as Clint joined him on the boardwalk.

"Jesse—"

"What the hell are you doing in Northfield?"

"Trying to keep you from making a big mistake—"

"This sure is a coincidence, running into—"

"Jesse, shut up and listen! This is not the bank to rob, do you hear me? If you try it this whole town will come down on you."

Jesse immediately knew that Clint was telling him the truth.

"I had a bad feeling about this one," he said, "but nobody would listen to me."

"They should have, Jesse," Clint said. "They should have listened."

They were looking at each other when they heard the barrage of shots.

Cole Younger was usually the man who went inside and was in charge of things. He knew things could go bad without warning, and he wanted to try to prevent that. He and Miller rushed to the bank. The other three had entered and had left the door open.

"Clell, get inside and close the door!"

Miller obeyed, rushing to the bank, entering and closing the door.

So he wouldn't look conspicuous Cole pretended he was checking the cinch on his saddle.

A man named J. S. Allen, who owned a store on one side of the bank, became suspicious and walked over to the bank. As he tried to enter, however, Clell Miller barred his way.

"Can't go in," he said.

"Why not?"

"Closed."

"The bank is never closed at this hour."

"Then it's too crowded."

"What do you mean?" Allen tried to look past Miller.

"Get out of here, friend!" Miller said between his teeth. "I mean it."

Allen backed away and walked from the bank. Inside Frank, Bob, and Pitts had tellers filling up bags with money. Miller stayed on the door.

Allen wasted no time. As soon as he turned the corner he started shouting, "They're robbing the bank, they're robbing the bank!"

Across the street a young man on the porch of the Dampier House Hotel took up the cry. "Robbery, robbery!"

"Shut up!" Cole shouted. "Mind your own business." But he knew it was too late. He pulled his gun and fired a warning shot into the air. He was warning the men in the bank, and Jesse and Jim, wherever they were.

The next shots came from inside the bank, and all hell broke loose.

TWENTY-SIX

Jesse ran for his horse at the sound of the shots, with Jim Younger right behind him. They both had brothers in danger.

"Jesse, wait!" Clint shouted, afraid that his friend was running headlong into certain death.

Later Clint was able to reconstruct everything that happened from the time Jesse rode off. . . .

Jesse and Jim Younger rode up to the bank, firing their guns and shouting at the top of their lungs. They were trying to distract attention from the rest of the gang, who were either in the bank, or in front of it.

A pedestrian by the name of Nicholas Gustavson, an immigrant who didn't know what was going on, was struck by a stray bullet and killed.

The citizens of Northfield were ready to defend their town, and their bank. As Clell Miller came out of the bank and made for his horse, an old-timer, who had fought in many Indian wars, fired a blast of bird shot into his face.

Another man killed Charlie Pitts's horse.

Cole was shouting to the outlaws in the back that it was time to get out. As he was doing so he was suddenly hit in the thigh by a bullet.

Off to the side Bill Chadwell was hit in the heart with a

shot and died instantly. This was bad news, because he was the local boy, and now—if the outlaws escaped—they'd have to find their way out of Minnesota without him.

Clint came upon the scene at this point but didn't dare get any closer, and couldn't take part. If he took the outlaws' part he'd become an outlaw himself, and he'd have to shoot at innocent citizens who were just protecting what was theirs.

If he fought on the side of the citizens he might have to kill one of his friends, Frank or Jesse. He could only watch and wait to see what the outcome would be.

Suddenly, someone was firing from a window in the Dampier House Hotel. Whoever it was missed with his first shot, but his second shot struck Clell Miller—already wounded from the bird shot in his face—killing him instantly.

Clint saw Bob Younger come running from the bank, and then saw him spin as he was hit in the right elbow. Bob switched his gun to his left hand but could not maintain his hold on the bag of money he had, and let it fall to the ground.

Cole Younger had managed to mount his horse, and now Bob ran up to him and swung up behind him.

Frank James had managed to get from the bank to his horse without being injured, and he and Jesse rode hell-bent for leather out of town. Oddly, the armed townspeople did not fire after the fleeing outlaws, else Frank and Jesse might have also been wounded.

The sheriff came running onto the scene at this point and spotted Clint.

"What the hell happened?"

"Bank robbery."

"Who tried to rob the bank?"

"Damned if I know," Clint said. "I didn't see them."

"Didn't you try to help?"

Clint spread his hands in a helpless gesture.

"I came on the scene too late, Sheriff, but your citizens seem to have handled it all right."

"I'd better check and see if anybody in the bank got hurt."

As it turned out, one of the bank employees, who tried to escape, had been wounded in the shoulder by Charlie Pitts. Another, Joseph Haywood, the head bookkeeper, had been shot and killed almost as an afterthought, the witnesses said. The outlaws were on their way out of the bank, and one of them turned and deliberately shot the man in the chest, killing him instantly.

The only money that had been taken was from the teller's window because the outlaws had been lied to about the vault being on a time lock. Bob Younger had dropped that bag of money when he was shot, so the outlaws had not gotten away with a cent.

TWENTY-SEVEN

Left without their guide, because Chadwell had been killed, the outlaws wandered for a good five days while search parties and posses were out looking for them. Somewhere near a town called Mankato they found an abandoned farmhouse and took refuge there until they could figure out what to do.

As luck would have it, Frank and Jesse had escaped from Northfield unscathed while two of the Youngers, Bob and Cole, had been injured.

Cole's thigh injury hindered his riding, which kept it from healing, but his injury was still not as serious as Bob's. Jesse felt that Bob's wound had shattered his elbow, and had become infected, and he was in favor of leaving Bob behind, because he expected him to die. This infuriated Cole, and they started to fight.

"You're a no-good bastard to even suggest that, Jesse," Cole said. "Bob's my brother, I ain't leavin' him. I ought to kill you for what you said."

"Frank thinks so, too," Jesse said.

Frank turned his head.

"I don't have a problem with Frank," Cole said. "He and I have always been friends, but you and me are through."

"That's fine by me," Jesse said. "Frank will have to make up his own mind what he wants to do."

They finally decided that Frank and Jesse would go their own way, and Charlie Pitts and the Youngers would go theirs.

The Youngers and Pitts did not get very far. They were surrounded by a posse near Madelia and, in a firefight, Pitts was killed and each of the Youngers was wounded many times. However, even though Jim was shot five times, and Cole was shot eleven times, and Bob was shot in the lung, they all survived and were sentenced to prison in Faribault, Minnesota. They pleaded guilty to avoid execution and were sentenced to life imprisonment.

TWENTY-EIGHT

After the gang left Northfield Clint wasn't sure what he should do. He thought about getting Duke and going after them, but for what? Frank and Jesse had not been wounded—not that he had seen—so they didn't need his help in that respect. He didn't know how well the James brothers or the Youngers knew Minnesota, so maybe they could have used his help as a guide.

Actually, the decision was made for him when Sheriff Raiford approached him later that afternoon at his hotel.

"I've got witnesses who saw you talking to Jesse James," Raiford said.

"What?"

"You heard me."

Clint's first instinct was to lie about it, but then he decided not to.

"So? Is there a law against talking to Jesse James?" he asked.

"There's a law against aiding and abetting a fugitive."

"As you said," Clint replied, "I was talking to him, I wasn't aiding or abetting."

"Adams, I've never heard anything about you ever holding up a bank or a train. I'm gonna ask you now, are you or have you ever been a member of the James gang?"

"No."

"Be that as it may," Raiford said, "I still think you should leave Northfield."

"Is this about Fay?"

"This is not about Fay," Raiford said, "this is about me doing my job."

"Fine. I'll leave."

"I want you to do one thing before you do."

"What's that?"

"Have a look at the outlaws that were killed and identify them."

Clint agreed to do that and identified Clell Miller and Bill Chadwell. After that was done he said good-bye to Fay and left Northfield approximately eighteen hours after the James-Younger gang did.

The trail had been trampled by a posse made up of townspeople who could not read sign. However, Clint was still able to pick it out and follow it.

He lost it several times over the next few days, and at one point almost decided to pack it in and head out of Minnesota himself. But thinking of Frank and Jesse wandering aimlessly around, when the weather was getting cold, he kept going. It took him six days to find the farmhouse where they had taken refuge. From the amount of blood he found he reckoned that somebody was badly wounded. He remembered seeing Bob Younger take a bullet in the right arm, but he hadn't seen any of the others get hit. That didn't mean they hadn't, though. For all he knew they had all been wounded.

Leaving the house were two sets of tracks. Six horses all together, two going off in one direction, four in another. Since there were three Youngers and at least one other gang member, he decided that the set of two tracks going off on their own had to be Frank and Jesse, and he followed those.

Frank and Jesse found themselves wandering aimlessly in unfamiliar territory. Adding to their difficulty was the fact that Jesse was upset with Frank for not backing him when he vetoed the Northfield job, and Frank was upset with Jesse for wanting to leave Bob Younger behind.

Once, outside of Lake Crystal, they came upon a deputy who started firing at them immediately. Both their horses spooked and threw them, but in the dark they managed to get away.

Now they were on foot and they needed horses as well as food.

They found a farmhouse and stole two horses. Riding south they decided to split up and meet in Fort Dodge.

Jesse found his way to a farmhouse where the people—a farmer, his wife, and three sons—were hospitable and took him in for a few days.

Frank kept traveling until, finally, he and Clint ran into each other.

TWENTY-NINE

"This is exactly why I hate coincidences," Clint said, as Frank walked into his camp.

"Son of a bitch," Frank said. "I saw the fire, but I'd've never guessed it was you."

"Sit down, I'll get you something to eat."

Frank sat across the fire from Clint and accepted a cup of coffee. He sipped it while Clint scraped some beans onto a plate.

"Thanks," Frank said. "I'm pretty hungry."

"What happened, Frank?" Clint asked. "What went wrong in Northfield?"

"Lots of things," Frank said. "First, Jesse was right, the job didn't feel good. I should have backed him when he said he didn't want to do it."

"Why didn't you?"

"Chadwell said it was a rich bank," Frank said. "I thought this could be my last job."

"You want to quit?"

Frank nodded.

"Been wanting to for a long time, Clint. Ever since I got married. Ever since the Huntington job. This is no life for Annie."

"And Jesse?"

"Jesse wants to keep going. He's still got things to prove."

"But he didn't want to do Northfield."

"No."

"What happened in the bank?"

Frank finished his beans and put the plate down. He passed a hand over his face, then held out his coffee cup to Clint.

"How about some more?"

"Sure."

Clint poured the cup full.

"I messed up in Northfield," he said then. "Bob had a bottle, he started passing it around. I never should've had anything to drink. I wasn't drunk, not exactly, but I wasn't in the right frame of mind. Bob, he *was* drunk, and he shot one of the tellers who was trying to get out. Didn't have to happen. And then the town . . ."

"The town takes care of its own," Clint said. "I learned that the few days I was in Northfield."

"Why were you there?"

"I was passing through, Frank," he said. "Just passing through."

"Like that first time, huh? When you pulled my bacon out of the fire outside of St. Genevieve?"

Clint decided it was time to tell the truth about that time.

"I wasn't passing through then, Frank," Clint said. "I was looking for you and Jesse. I was working for the Pinkertons."

Frank stared at Clint for a few moments, then laughed and shook his head.

"So Jesse had that right, too, huh?"

"Jesse knew?"

"He figured."

"Why didn't he try to kill me?"

"He said he knew you'd never last with the Pinkertons. You weren't their type."

"I wasn't really with the Pinkertons, just doing a job here

and there," Clint said, "but Jesse was right. I didn't last much longer."

"Why didn't you bring them down on us?"

"Well, for one thing I didn't save your life just to turn you in," Clint said.

"And for another?"

"I just plain liked you boys."

They drank coffee in silence for a while. Clint studied Frank, found him thin, drawn.

"Where's Jesse, Frank?"

"We split up. We're gonna meet in Fort Dodge."

"Was he hit?"

"No."

"You?"

Frank looked down at himself and said, "No, I'm all right. Cole and Bob, they were hit, Bob pretty bad."

"Why'd you all split at the farmhouse?"

"You found that place?"

"Yes. I think I was there the day after you. There were two separate sets of tracks."

"Cole and Jesse had a fight, almost came to blows."

"About what?"

"Jesse wanted to leave Bob behind. Said he was gonna die, anyway."

"Cole didn't like that."

"Not one bit. Said he should kill Jesse for suggesting it. I thought they were both gonna go for their guns. Cole said he and Jesse were through."

"And you?"

"I—I backed Jesse, even though I knew he was wrong. We rode with Cole and Bob and Jim a long time, Clint. Jesse never should have said that about leaving Bob behind."

"Why did he?"

"I don't know," Frank said. "He was pretty upset with Bob's drinking before Northfield. Maybe he blamed the whole thing on Bob. I don't know. I was as much to blame as Bob was."

"Somebody gunned down a man in cold blood as you boys left the bank," Clint said. "Who did that?"

"That was Chadwell. Is he dead?"

Clint nodded.

"Him and Clell Miller."

Frank rubbed his face again.

"You know, after Huntington, West Virginia, went bad we didn't go out on a job for a year."

Clint knew that Frank had gone with Cole and a man called Tom Webb to rob a bank in Huntington, a job Jesse didn't want to go on. It was the first time Frank had gone on a job without Jesse, and that one went bad.

"Things haven't been the same between me and Jesse, Clint," Frank said, "and after Northfield . . . I just don't know."

"If you want to quit, Frank, you should quit."

"What if Jesse goes out on a job without me and gets killed? What would I tell Ma?"

"How is your ma?"

"Ain't seen her in a while," Frank said. "They had to take that arm off, you know, after the bombing."

"I know."

"We never did thank you for what you did that night, did we? Me and Jesse? Not proper, anyway."

"Forget it."

"You done a lot for us, Clint."

"I'm going to do more, Frank."

"What are you going to do?"

"Show you the way out of Minnesota."

In the morning Frank and Clint split up, Clint making sure that Frank knew how to get to Fort Dodge to meet up with Jesse.

"What are you going to do?" he asked Frank before they rode in separate directions.

"I'm not sure," Frank said. "I guess I got to think about it some more."

"Doesn't sound like you'll ever ride with Cole and the others again."

"I know."

"With Chadwell and Miller gone you'd have to put together a whole new crew."

"I know that, too."

"If your heart's not in it anymore, Frank," Clint said, "then you *should* quit."

Frank reached out and clutched Clint's shoulder for a moment, then wheeled his horse around and rode away. Clint watched him until he was out of sight, and wondered if he'd ever see Frank and Jesse James again.

THIRTY

Back to the present, on the train from Kearney to St. Joe, Zee James stared at Clint as he finished his story.

"If Jesse wanted to leave Bob behind," she said finally, "he must have thought it was the right thing to do."

"Zee," Clint said, "when did Jesse ever do what was right? I mean, he was an outlaw, right? That's not something he ever denied. Don't you do it, now that he's dead."

"You're not listening," Zee replied. "I said he must have *thought* it was the right thing to do. I was married to Jesse, Clint, but that doesn't mean I was blind. I know he and Frank and Cole and the others broke the law. I didn't always agree with everything Jesse said and did. I wasn't just the dutiful wife, you know. I have a mind of my own."

"I know that, Zee," Clint said. "I'm sorry if I sounded like I didn't."

"Your story does explain a lot," she said. "I knew for a long time that Frank wanted to stop. He'd go away between jobs, but every time Jesse called him, he'd come."

"The older brother," Clint said, "watching out for the younger."

"And now he feels responsible for Jesse's death."

"Frank?"

She nodded.

"He thinks if he'd been around this wouldn't have happened."

"And what did his mother tell him? And you?"

"I haven't seen Frank, Clint," she said, "but Ma has. She can't talk to him, though. She says he won't listen."

"Did she arrange for me to talk to him?"

"She's trying. She'll contact us in St. Joe if she gets him to agree."

"What's he planning, Zee?"

"According to Ma," she said, "he's going to try to kill Bob and Charley Ford."

"That's crazy," Clint said. "The law will be waiting for him."

"That's what Ma tried to tell him."

"He'll go walking right into a trap."

"I don't think he cares, Clint."

"Well, I care, damn it," Clint said. "I told him once before I didn't save his life to see him get killed."

"I don't know if even you will be able to talk him out of it."

"I guess we'll have to wait and find out."

When the train pulled into St. Joe, Clint walked Zee back to the house where she lived as Zee Howard. She'd had a garden in front, but apparently, in their absence, people had come by for mementos, and had picked the garden almost clean.

"Why stay here, Zee?" he asked as he walked her to the door.

She turned and looked at her decimated garden.

"I don't know, Clint," she said. "I don't know what to do. Ma wants me to come to Kearney with the kids."

"Then do it."

"I'll have to think about it," she said. "I'm just so tired right now."

"Get some rest," he said as she opened her door.

Impulsively, she turned and gave him a quick hug, then went inside.

He left the Howard house and walked back to the hotel. As he approached it he saw Sheriff Timberlake standing out front. Apparently it hadn't taken long for the word to get back to the lawman that he and Zee were back in St. Joe.

''Can we talk, Adams?'' Timberlake asked.

''Sure, Sheriff,'' Clint said, ''how about inside?''

''Fine,'' the lawman said, and followed him in.

THIRTY-ONE

Clint led Timberlake into the hotel dining room. After all the talking with Zee on the train he was dry. He would have preferred a beer, but that would come later. Right now a cup of coffee and a piece of pie sounded good.

"Coffee?" Clint asked Timberlake as the waiter approached.

"Uh, yeah, sure."

"Two coffees. Pie?"

"No, thanks."

"Peach pie."

"Yes, sir."

Timberlake was in his forties, a big, barrel-chested man who had been sheriff in St. Joe for some time. Clint knew that the man was often at odds with Henry Craig, the police commissioner of Kansas City, but he knew from the inquest that they had worked in tandem on this whole Jesse James thing, along with Governor Crittenden.

"What's on your mind, Sheriff?"

"Frank James."

"What about him?"

"I want him to give himself up."

"Why come to me about that?"

"You're friends with him," Timberlake said. "You were friends with him and Jesse."

"So?"

"So you can convince him to give himself up."

"Sheriff," Clint said, "right now I'd have a hard time trying to convince him not to kill everyone who was involved in this fiasco, from the governor on down to that little weasel, Bob Ford."

Timberlake sat back as the waiter came with the coffee and Clint's pie.

Once the waiter left he said, "Look, I can't say that I approve of the way we went about this. It was Crittenden's idea, and he made the deal with the Fords' sister."

"Are they still in jail?"

"Right now, yes."

"But not for long, right?" Clint asked. "That was their deal with the governor?"

"I . . . really can't comment on that, Adams."

"Look, Sheriff," Clint said, "right now the safest place for the Fords is in jail. It's probably also your best bet for catching Frank, if he decided to come for them."

"He wouldn't try to come right into the jail after them, would he?"

"And he'd probably kill whoever was there with them."

This made the lawman look uncomfortable.

"You got to talk to him, Adams," Timberlake said. "Tell him I'm sorry about what happened with his brother. It wasn't my idea."

"But you went along with it."

"I didn't have a choice. It was my job."

"To arrange to have a man shot in the back, and then give the man who did it amnesty? I'd have turned in my badge rather than go along with something like that, Timberlake."

Clint took a taste of his pie and then pushed it away. He'd lost his appetite. In fact, right at that moment he wanted that beer he'd been thinking about.

He stood up.

"Where are you going?"

"To the saloon," Clint said. "If you want to talk to me any more, that's where I'll be."

Clint was standing at the bar with a half finished beer when Timberlake came walking in slowly. It was early, and the place wasn't doing much business.

"Beer, Sheriff?" the bartender asked.

"Uh, no, thanks."

The bartender shrugged and moved down the bar.

"Adams, look, I don't want the same thing that happened to Jesse to happen to Frank."

"I can't see why not."

"Why won't you believe that this has left a bad taste in my mouth?"

"Because you should have thought of that before you went along with it," Clint said.

"Yeah, you're right, I probably should have, but I didn't. I wanted to keep my job."

"Well, good, you did that. Now you'll have to deal with Frank."

"Has—has he got another gang? I mean, I know they were trying to recruit Bob and Charley, that's how they got into the house, but—"

"There's no more James gang, Sheriff," Clint said. "Jesse was the leader, and would have been the leader, of any gang. With him dead, there's no more gang."

"But Frank—"

"Frank doesn't want to head a gang," Clint said. "I'm sure all he's thinking about now is avenging his brother's death."

"By going after the Fords?"

Clint couldn't resist.

"He'll probably start there, since Bob was the one who pulled the trigger, but who knows who he'll go after next."

"You talk to him, Adams," Timberlake said. "You tell him everything I said."

"If I see him, Sheriff," Clint said, "I'll be sure to tell him you're real sorry."

THIRTY-TWO

Clint stayed in the saloon for the better part of the day. He left only long enough to go back to the hotel to let the clerk know where he was in case someone was looking for him.

He wondered if he should go and look for Frank instead of waiting for Frank to find him. Of course, there was no guarantee that Frank would come looking for him. If his mother couldn't convince him to talk to Clint, then he could be waiting a long time in that saloon.

He thought again about what had happened between him and Zee, and hoped that it would always stay buried and never be told. He knew he was never going to tell anyone; now all he had to do was hope that Zee never felt guilty enough to tell. Not that he was ashamed of it. He'd decided that he wasn't, and that it would always be a sweet memory for him. He hoped it would be for her, too.

He thought about Timberlake. The man was probably a good lawman who got caught in a bad situation. After all, Crittenden was the governor. When he told Police Commissioner Craig and Sheriff Timberlake what he wanted them to do, they probably had to do it in order to hold on to their jobs. Clint just didn't think he could ever have a job he wanted to hold on to that badly.

Clint had taken his third beer—or was it his fourth—to a

back table as the saloon began to fill up, and that's where he was when he saw Ben Morrow walk into the saloon. He didn't particularly want to talk to Morrow, but the man seemed intent on finding him, and when he did he came walking over.

"Mind if I sit?"

"Do we have to pretend we know each other?"

"Naw," Morrow said, sitting down, " 'cause we do."

"Why are you here, Ben?"

"I got a message for you."

"From Frank?"

"Not directly," he said. "This comes from Mrs. Samuels."

"And?"

"She says Frank don't want to talk to you."

"She's got to convince him to."

"She's still working on it."

"Well," Clint said, "if that's the case then he must still be in Kearney."

"I guess."

"Ben, what do you think Frank will do?"

"He's gonna kill Bob Ford. Charley, too, probably."

"He tell you that?"

"I ain't talked to him, Clint, but ain't that what you'd do if Jesse was your brother?"

"If I were Frank," Clint said, "probably."

"You gonna be here all night?"

Clint frowned at the beer in front of him. He'd lost count already. He pushed it away.

"No," he said, "I'm leaving now."

"Where you gonna be?"

"After I talk to Timberlake, I'll be at my hotel."

"Why are you gonna talk to him?"

"Because," Clint said, standing up, "I just got an idea."

"Move 'em? Where?" Timberlake asked.

"I don't know," Clint said. "Anywhere. Move them where Frank can't get at them."

"I can't move Bob and Charley on my own," Timberlake said. "The governor said—"

"The governor isn't here, Timberlake, and you are. He's not the one who might catch a bullet when Frank comes to get the Fords, you are."

"Well," Timberlake said, "I suppose I could send a telegram to Commissioner Craig, in Kansas City. If he'll take them, Frank couldn't possibly get at them there."

"That's good thinking, Timberlake," Clint said, "real good thinking."

"I'd better send it now."

"Another good idea."

"Is Frank in town?"

"No," Clint said, "not that I know of, which is all the more reason you should get this done before he does come to town, don't you think?"

"Uh, yeah, I do," Timberlake said, standing and grabbing his hat. "I sure do."

Clint returned to his hotel room, removed his boots and reclined on the bed. He was tired, and there was no harm in taking a nap. He wanted to be where Ben Morrow could find him, just in case Frank did agree to see him. He also wanted to be where Timberlake could find him, just in case he got the okay to move the Fords somewhere else.

What could he possibly tell Frank that would change his mind about killing the Fords? Frank always had that older brother mentality, and right now he felt that he had failed his little brother. Could Clint convince him otherwise? Tell him that Jesse would have come to this end anyway, if he hadn't settled down? Would Frank buy that at all?

Would he, if Jesse were his brother?

THIRTY-THREE

A knock on the door woke him and he groped for his gun on the bedpost. He'd slept too soundly. If somebody had wanted to kill him, he'd be dead now. He got off the bed and went to the door.

"Who is it?"

"It's Zee, Clint."

He opened the door and let her in.

"What are you doing here, Zee?" he demanded.

"What do you think I'm doin' here?"

"Look, I don't—"

"Frank has agreed to see you."

"Where? When?"

"Outside of town, about three miles north, there's an old cabin. He'll be there."

"When?"

"Two hours from now."

"All right," Clint said. "I'll go and see him. You'd better go back home."

She went to the door, then stopped before opening it.

"Why did you think I was here, Clint?"

"Why else?" he asked. "To tell me about Frank."

"Good," she said, and left.

Clint went to the pitcher and basin on the dresser and

washed his face. He'd been careless a handful of times in his life, and this was one of them. Luckily, he'd survived them all, but the older he got the *less* careless he had to get, not more.

He pulled on his boots, strapped on his gun, and went out to have a meal before he went to meet Frank.

By the time he followed Zee's directions and reached the cabin it was dark. There was no light showing in the cabin as he rode up to it. He considered briefly that it might be some kind of a trap, but then pushed that from his mind. For one thing, Zee wouldn't have been a party to that, and for another, who would set a trap for him now? The only people he was involved with were the James family, and the law.

Then again, look what the law had cooked up for Jesse James.

He rode up to the cabin and dismounted.

"Frank?"

"In here." Frank's voice came from inside the cabin. "Are you alone?"

"Of course I'm alone. Come on, Frank, we have to talk. Do you have a light in there?"

There was a moment of silence and then Clint heard a match being struck, and the inside of the cabin was bathed in light.

"Come on in."

Clint walked into the cabin, which was bare and empty—except for Frank James, a lighted lantern at his feet. Clint couldn't believe his eyes. Frank was as thin as a skeleton, and looked years older than when he'd last seen him—more years than he should have.

"Frank—"

"I know," Frank said, "I look like shit. Did you bring any food?"

"I didn't know—I have some beef jerky in my saddle-bags, and a canteen."

"I'd be obliged."

Clint went and got them and handed them to Frank.

"How's Zee?" Frank asked.

Clint was surprised at how guilty he felt when Frank asked the question.

"She's fine," Clint said, "holding up."

"She's a good woman," Frank said. "She deserved better than what she got from Jesse. Annie deserves better than what she gets from me."

"They love you, Frank—"

"That don't matter," Frank said. "Ma loved us, now she's got one hand instead of two."

"That wasn't—"

"Jesse and me, we loved each other, and now he's dead because I wasn't here."

"I think you got that wrong, Frank."

"Is that why Ma and Zee wanted me to talk to you?" Frank asked. "So you could tell me it wasn't my fault?"

"So I could talk some sense into you, maybe."

"The only thing that makes sense," Frank said, "is killing Bob Ford—Charley, too."

"And who else after them?"

"Whoever was involved with killin' Jesse."

"That means Sheriff Timberlake, Commissioner Craig—"

"Them, too."

"And Governor Crittenden," Clint said. "You prepared to assassinate the governor of the state, Frank?"

"If I have to."

"And who says whether you have to or not?"

He swallowed some jerky and washed it down with a swig of water.

"I say," Frank said. "I say which of them lives and which of them dies."

"That makes you God, I guess."

"Ain't no God," Frank said. "I used to believe there was, but not no more."

"What happened, Frank?" Clint asked. "What happened since I saw you last, in Minnesota?"

"Jesse," Frank said, "he just got crazier and crazier. I had to get away from him."

"But whenever he called for you, you came, Frank."

"Of course I came. He's my brother—he *was* my brother. I—I had to come."

"And then when the job was done?"

"I had to get away again."

"Frank," Clint said, "you always took too much on yourself."

"Not enough," Frank said. "If I had took enough he wouldn't be dead."

"Frank, Jesse was going to come to this end no matter what you did," Clint said. "What you should have done a long time ago was think about saving yourself. That's what you should do now."

"I'll save myself," Frank said, "when I'm done avenging Jesse."

"Frank—"

"They think there was blood before?" Frank said. "Wait until they see what happens now."

"Frank—"

"No!" Frank shouted, and kicked the lantern. It shattered and flames shot across the floor and climbed up the wall. Clint got out of the cabin, which went up like a tinderbox, and he assumed that Frank had gotten out some back way.

At least, he hoped he had.

THIRTY-FOUR

To satisfy himself that Frank had gotten out of the burning cabin, Clint remained there until the small cabin had literally burned to the ground. He moved Duke back from the flames, so he wouldn't get agitated. When he didn't see a body among the charred embers he mounted and rode back to St. Joe, thoroughly unsatisfied with his meeting with Frank James.

"Mr. Adams," the desk clerk called as he entered the hotel lobby.

"Yes?"

As Clint got close the clerk caught the burning smell that had affixed itself to Clint and his clothes.

"Oh, uh, the sheriff was looking for you. He asked that you come and see him when you got back."

"It's late," Clint said. "Will he be in his office?"

"He said to tell you that as long as he had the Fords in jail, he would be at his office."

"Okay, thanks."

"Are you, uh, all right, sir?"

"I've got to stop smoking," Clint said, and left the hotel.

He went to the sheriff's office, found the door locked, and knocked loudly. After a few moments it was unlocked and Sheriff Timberlake opened it.

"Oh, good, it's you. Come on in."

Clint entered and Timberlake closed the door behind him.

"I've got some coffee going. You want some?"

"Sure, thanks."

"Whew," the lawman said, "you smell like . . . firewood. Where've you been?"

"I met with Frank," Clint said, reaching out to accept the cup of coffee. The sheriff almost spilled it, recovered, and handed it to him.

Clint told Timberlake about his meeting with Frank, and the fire.

"And he got out?"

"Yes, Sheriff, he got out," Clint said. "He's still alive."

"And still after the Fords?"

"He hasn't changed his mind. What progress did you make in getting them moved?"

"None."

"Why not?"

"You know why not."

"They're being used as bait to catch Frank."

Timberlake nodded.

"Do they know it?"

"No, and I ain't about to tell 'em."

"Who's springing this little trap?"

"Craig."

"Marshal, or commissioner?"

"The commissioner," Timberlake said. "He's already got men in town. He says he won't move the Fords until he's good and ready."

"And he's got the governor's blessing on this?"

"That's what he says."

"Damn."

"What are you gonna do, Adams?"

"All I can do is wait, just like everybody else, Sheriff."

"You've got the kind of gun that makes a difference, Adams. If Frank tries anything—"

"I won't shoot at Frank, Sheriff."

"And what about the law?"

Clint shook his head.

"I won't fire at anyone wearing a badge either—unless they fire at me."

"And there's no reason for that to happen, is there?" Timberlake asked.

Clint shook his head and said, "Not that I know of."

THIRTY-FIVE

Clint went to see Zee next, but he left it until morning, after he'd had a bath to get the burning stench off his skin, and then some breakfast.

"I've been waiting for you," she said as she let him into the house. Somewhere in another room he heard the sound of children playing.

"How are they taking it?" he asked.

She shrugged and said, "They're children. When they get bored they look around for him. Do you want some coffee?"

"Yes."

"Come in the kitchen and tell me what happened last night." She led the way. "Did you meet with Frank?"

"I did."

"And?"

Briefly, he told her about his conversation with her brother-in-law and how it had turned out.

"It burned down?"

"Yes."

"Did he—"

"He got out."

"Are you sure?"

"I waited a long time to be able to find out," he said. "Yes, I'm sure."

She handed him a cup of black coffee.

"It might have been better if he hadn't."

Clint didn't reply, but he knew what she meant.

"So now what happens?"

"I've talked to the sheriff about getting the Fords moved."

"And?"

"The commissioner in Kansas City won't allow it."

"They're going to use them to catch Frank, aren't they?"

"Yes," Clint said. "Apparently there are already some men in town for that purpose."

"He won't care," she said. "He'll die trying to kill Bob Ford."

"Not if I can help it."

"What can you do? Save his life? Again? How?"

"I don't know yet," Clint said. "I'm working on it."

"You can only do so much, Clint," Zee said. "You should leave town. Just go. You've done enough for the James family. If you stay you might get shot, or get in trouble with the law."

"I can't just leave, Zee," he said. "I've got to see this through."

"Why?"

He sat down, and she sat across from him.

"I've been crossing paths with the James boys my whole life," Clint said. "I think I was supposed to be here, at the end."

"Then if you stay," she said, "you have to keep it from being the end. You have to keep Frank from dying."

"I know," he said. "I know."

"But he won't listen," she said, banging her fist on the table. "He won't listen to anyone."

"Where would he be, Zee?" Clint asked. "You've been around them for years. Where would he be?"

She thought a moment, then said, "The caves."

"What caves?"

"The caves that Frank and Jesse and the others used as a hideout."

"And they're near here?"

"Yes."

"Do you know where?"

"Not exactly," she said. "I—I've never been there, I just heard Jesse talk about them."

"Tell me what he said, then," Clint said. "Take your time and tell me everything you remember that might have something to do with the caves."

For the next fifteen minutes she wracked her brain and kept talking while Clint listened and sifted through it all for a hint, a clue, about where Frank James might be.

THIRTY-SIX

When Clint left the "Howard" house he still didn't know where Frank was, but he had an idea of where to look. Before he did that, though, he wanted to check out the town and see if he could spot the men Commissioner Craig had sent from Kansas City.

By midday he thought he had half a dozen men identified as marshals or deputies or some kind of lawmen. They might even have been Pinkertons. He wondered if his message had been carried back to Allan, and how he might react to it. It would be just like Pinkerton to respond by sending men to St. Joe, rather than staying away. He was as stubborn a cuss as Clint had ever met, and getting worse as he got older.

By late afternoon he was convinced if Frank rode into St. Joe he'd have no chance to ever get near the jail, where the Ford boys were being held. He'd be committing suicide just by riding down the main street. Clint was sure that some trigger-happy lawman—or Pinkerton looking to impress his boss—would shoot Frank James on sight.

Which made it all the more imperative that he find him.

Clint rode out of St. Joe that afternoon, even though he knew he had less than three hours of daylight left. He could have waited until the next day, but his assessment of the force that

Commissioner Craig had sent to St. Joe made him uneasy about waiting.

He followed Zee's directions to an area outside of town that had some hill caves. She said Jesse had used them quite a few times as a hideout, and that Frank might be doing that now.

After two and a half hours of searching he was ready to give up and go back when he got an idea. If he waited until *after* dark maybe a light from inside a cave might give Frank's location away. After all Frank would need a fire not only for light, but for heat, as well.

He spent the next half hour just riding around, checking the ground for sign, and then darkness began to fall. When it did he dismounted and walked Duke. He didn't want to take a chance on injuring the big gelding in the dark.

After an hour and a half of walking around, he was starting to think he was wasting his time when he saw it. It was a flicker, and he almost missed it. He backed up a bit and saw it again. He realized that the light could only be seen from this angle. He was just glad he was the one seeing it, and not one of Craig's or Pinkerton's men.

He walked toward the glow, then dropped Duke's reins to the ground, confident that the horse would still be there when he came out.

He advanced toward the mouth of the cave and could see the glow clearly now. He entered, wondering if he'd find some hermit instead of Frank James.

"Frank?"

No answer.

"Come on, Frank? Are you in here? I can see the glow of the fire from outside."

No reply.

"Real careless of you, Frank."

After a long moment a voice said, "Yeah, well, Jesse was the smart one."

"Can I come in?"

"Come ahead."

Clint moved deeper into the cave and found Frank sitting in a cavern at a fire. He could smell coffee and beans.

"Well, at least the smell isn't getting outside," he said.

"Sit down," Frank said. "My turn to feed you."

Clint sat across the fire from Frank, who still looked charred—or just plain dirty—and smelled from the fire.

"Where'd you get the food?"

"A farmer," Frank said. "We still got friends in the area."

Frank handed Clint a cup of coffee and a plate of beans.

"I didn't think you could see the fire from outside," he said.

"Just a glimpse from the right angle," Clint said.

"What are you doin' out here?"

"Looking for you," Clint said around a mouthful of beans. Some bacon would have made them tastier but that smell probably would have extended outside the cave.

"No, I mean, how did you know where to look?"

"Zee."

"Oh."

"She's worried about you."

"She don't need to worry."

"I'm worried, too."

"Why?"

"The town is crawling with extra law," Clint said. "They're just waiting for you to come in after the Fords."

"They'll have a long wait."

"Why's that?"

"Jesse may have been the smart one, Clint," he said, "but that don't make me stupid."

"That's the second time you said that," Clint commented. "What makes you think Jesse was the smart one?"

"Well, wasn't he?"

"Who was the one who wanted to stop all the robbing, Frank? Who was the one who recognized that it was getting out of hand?"

"I never wanted to start it in the first place," Frank said. "Jesse talked me into it."

"That made him the more persuasive of the two of you," Clint said, "not the smartest."

"I guess you're right," Frank said, poking the fire with a stick so that it flared and crackled.

"So what did you mean when you said they'd have a long wait?" Clint put aside his now empty plate and held his cup out so Frank could refill it.

"I'm not dumb enough to try and take them in town," Frank said. "I'll wait until they transport them."

"What if they don't?"

"What do you mean?"

"What if they don't move them to another jail, or a prison? What if they just let them go?"

"That's fine by me, too," Frank said. "They'd be easier to take if they were released."

"After you take them, Frank," Clint asked, "what then?"

"I haven't thought that far ahead," Frank said. "Jesse used to do that, think far ahead."

"That made him a better planner," Clint said. "It still didn't make him smarter."

"You gonna head back to town tonight?"

"You inviting me to stay?"

"Why not?" Frank said. "Gets kind of lonely out here alone."

Clint looked around the cavern. In a corner was Frank's horse, and next to him his bedroll and saddle, but there wasn't much else in there.

"I'll go out and get Duke," Clint said, standing up. "Maybe you'd better make some more coffee."

"I'm way ahead of you," Frank said. "The way I figure it, you're gonna spend most of the night talkin' me out of goin' after Bob and Charley."

"And you said you were dumb."

"I never said that!" Frank shouted as Clint went outside to get Duke.

THIRTY-SEVEN

In the morning they made fresh coffee and some bacon. Clint commented on the smell of the bacon getting out of the cave.

"Don't matter," Frank said. "I ain't been stayin' in the same place two nights in a row."

"Where are you going to go tonight?"

"I don't know."

"You don't know," Clint asked, "or you don't want to tell me?"

Frank shrugged.

They had talked deep into the night, and Clint could see from the look on Frank's face that there was no way to talk the man out of seeking his revenge.

"You don't even have a plan," Clint said.

"Yes, I do," Frank said. "I'm gonna wait for Bob and Charley to leave St. Joe, and then I'm gonna kill 'em."

"And then what?"

"I told you," Frank said, "I don't plan that far ahead. That was Jesse's job."

"Well, now it's yours," Clint said. "If you don't plan ahead, you're just going to get yourself killed."

They ate and drank their coffee in silence for a few moments and then Frank said, "I got an idea."

"What?"

"You do it."

"I do what?"

"You plan it for us."

"Plan what, Frank?"

"You help me get Bob and Charley, and then help me get away."

"You want me to help you murder Bob and Charley Ford? That would make me as big an outlaw as you, Frank."

"Well, maybe not as big," Frank said. "Remember, Jesse and me been at this for some time now."

"Frank," Clint said, "you know me a long time. How did you think I'd react to that suggestion?"

Frank shrugged.

"It was just a thought," Frank said. "Jesse was your friend. I just thought you'd want to help."

"Of course I'd like to help," Clint said. "I'd like to help see that Bob and Charley get what they've got coming to them—"

"A bullet!"

"—in a court of law."

"Ain't no court gonna convict them of killin' Jesse, Clint," Frank said, shaking his head. "You know as well as me they got the governor on their side. They're gonna get off scot-free, and when they do I'm gonna be there."

"And there's no way I can talk you out of it?"

"You been tryin' all night, ain't you?" Frank asked. "Besides, you know me a long time. Did you think you could talk me out of it?"

"No."

"There ya go."

Frank stood up.

"Time for me to break camp and move on."

"Why? The law is just waiting in town for you."

"How long are they gonna wait before they come lookin'?"

"I don't know."

"Well, I'll keep movin', just the same."

"While you're at it," Clint said, "you might want to find a place to get a bath."

Frank sniffed himself.

"I know I'm kind of rank," he said, "but I wasn't expectin' company."

They both saddled their horses and walked them out of the camp.

"Do you need anything, Frank?" Clint asked. "Money? Food?"

"I can get what I need," Frank said. "The only thing I need from you is a plan."

"I tell you what," Clint said. "I'll try to come up with a plan that doesn't involve me killing anyone."

"But it gets me away after I do it?"

"Right."

"I can live with that."

"Where can I find you, then?"

Frank mounted up and looked down at Clint.

"I'll get word to Zee where I'm gonna be. You let her know when you got a plan set, and she'll get word to me. Then we'll plan to meet."

"Okay."

"When will you have this plan?"

"Give me a few days," Clint said. "I don't think anything is going to happen for a while."

Frank nodded.

"I knew you'd help me, Clint. You always do."

"Yeah," Clint said, not at all sure of what he was going to do.

"I'll talk to you soon."

"And you won't do anything until we talk again?"

"I promise," Frank said. "I won't make a move until I hear your plan."

"Good."

"I'll be seein' you," Frank said, then turned his horse and rode away. When he was out of sight Clint mounted Duke, turned him, and rode back to St. Joe.

THIRTY-EIGHT

"What kind of plan are you going to come up with?" Zee asked.

They were sitting in her kitchen again, and Clint found himself feeling uncomfortable *because* he felt comfortable there.

"I don't know, Zee," Clint said. "I was just talking, trying to get him to go along with me."

"So you never had a plan?"

"I'm not going to make a plan to help Frank kill somebody," he said. "You wouldn't want me to do that, would you?"

"You're asking the wrong person, Clint," she said bitterly. "I want Bob Ford dead as much as Frank does."

"But would you do it yourself? Would you be able to shoot him if you came face-to-face with him?"

"Yes," she said without hesitation, and he believed her. "Does that shock you? Or disappoint you?"

"No, Zee," Clint said, "neither of those. I understand how you feel."

"Do you?"

"No," he said honestly, "not completely."

He finished his coffee, and she removed their cups from the table, went to the sink, then turned and leaned against it.

"What will you do now?"

"I don't know what I can do," Clint said, "except . . ."

"Except what?"

"Well . . . I could go and talk to Bob and Charley."

"Why? What would you accomplish by doing that?"

He spread his hands helplessly.

"I don't know, but it's something to do, something I haven't done yet."

He stood up.

"Now?" she asked.

"Why not?"

"Will the sheriff let you in to see them?"

"There's only one way to find out."

She stared at something only she could see.

"I never thought of it."

"Thought of what?"

"Of going to see them in jail," she said, looking at him. "I never thought of it."

"What would that accomplish?"

"I don't know," she said, "but I'm coming with you."

"Zee—"

"I am," she said. "I'm coming with you."

He knew he couldn't talk her out of it, so he waited for her to get someone to watch the children, fetch her wrap, and then they walked to the jail together.

"You want to what?" Sheriff Timberlake asked.

"See the Fords," Clint said.

"Both of you?"

"Yes," Zee answered.

Timberlake sat back in his chair.

"I don't know—"

"Those men killed my husband, Sheriff," Zee said, cutting him off. "I have a right to see them."

Timberlake looked at Clint for help.

"I think she's right, Sheriff."

"And why do you want to see them?"

"I want to give them the good news."

"What good news?"

Clint smiled, because an idea had just come to him.

"I've talked Frank out of killing them."

Timberlake sat forward.

"You saw Frank?"

"I did."

"When?"

"Last night."

"Where?"

"In a cave outside of town."

"Those damn caves . . ." Timberlake said, shaking his head. "So Frank isn't gonna come into town?"

"No," Clint said. "That should disappoint Commissioner Craig in Kansas City, after he sent all those men here to lay a trap for Frank."

"I'll say . . . I mean . . ."

"Forget it, Sheriff," Clint said. "I've seen all the men. What I don't know is if they're marshals or Pinkertons."

"Both," Timberlake said.

"How about it, Sheriff?" Clint asked. "You going to let us see them?"

"Together, or separate?"

"Together," Clint said, and Zee nodded.

Timberlake sighed and stood up.

"All right," he said, snatching the keys to the cell area from the wall, "come with me."

Zee looked at Clint and took hold of his arm, squeezing it tightly. Within seconds she would be face-to-face with the men who came to her home, invited, and killed her husband.

She wished she had a gun.

THIRTY-NINE

"You got visitors, boys," Timberlake announced. He looked at Clint and said, "Five minutes."

"Thanks, Sheriff."

Timberlake withdrew. Charley Ford came to the front of the cell he was sharing with his brother. Neither of the Ford boys were happy. They had expected to be released and paid ten thousand dollars. This was what Governor Crittenden had promised. Instead, they'd been sitting in this cell for days, and hadn't been paid anything beyond an initial five hundred dollars they received.

Now Charley stared at Clint, not knowing who he was because they'd never met, but when he saw Zee he quickly backed away from the bars.

Zee, to her credit, stood in front of the cell and glared at the men inside, but didn't say a word.

"Bob," Charley said.

Bob looked up and saw Zee, and then Clint.

"Who are you?" he asked.

Clint was surprised again at how young Bob Ford looked.

"Clint Adams."

"The Gunsmith!" Charley said in awe. "He came here to kill us."

"He ain't got no gun," Bob said, which was true. Clint had given it to the sheriff.

"Why's he here, then?" Charley asked.

"Why don't you ask him?" Bob replied. "I'm more interested in why she's here."

"Miz James," Charley said, "I'm real sorry—"

"I don't want your apology!" she said, cutting him off. "I just came to look at the two cowards who shot my husband in the back, and to tell you that you still have to deal with Jesse's brother."

"I told you," Charley said to Bob. "I told you Frank would come after us."

"Maybe the Gunsmith is gonna come after us," Bob said. "How about it, Mr. Gunsmith? You hirin' out to kill us?"

"I wouldn't waste my time on you," Clint said.

"Then what are you doing here?"

"Same as Zee, I guess," Clint said. "Just wanted to take a look at the men who would shoot another man in the back."

"We wuz paid to do it," Charley said, as if the fault could be placed on the people who paid.

"That's no excuse," Clint said. "How much did you get?"

"Ten thousand," Charley said, before Bob could stop him.

Clint laughed.

"I'll bet you haven't seen a dime of that money yet."

"Have, too," Charley said. "Five hundred."

"Charley," Bob said, "you got to learn to shut up."

"Five hundred is all you'll ever see, boys," Clint said.

"That's what you say," Bob sneered.

"Look where you are, Bob," Clint said. "You were supposed to be out by now, weren't you?"

"We'll get out," Bob said with more self-assurance than he felt.

"And what happens when you do?" Clint asked.

"Frank kills them," Zee said. "That's what happens."

"That shows how much you know," Charley said. "Frank'll be dead or behind bars by then."

"Not a chance," Zee said.

"Why not?" Bob asked.

"Because we won't let either happen," she said.

"You and Adams?" Bob asked. "What can you do against federal marshals or Pinkertons?"

"Wait and see," Clint said.

He took Zee's arm and turned, as if to leave.

"Hey, Adams," Bob called. "Wait."

Clint nodded to Zee, who stepped back into the sheriff's office.

"Yeah?"

"Why'd you come here?"

"I told you," Clint said, "to look at a couple of cowards."

"I ain't no coward," Bob Ford said.

"Any man who shoots another man in the back is a coward, in my book."

"Well, you was at the inquest," Bob said. "You heard how we told it."

"I heard how you lied," Clint said. "The man had a hole in the back of his head. How do you explain that?"

"He, uh, turned just as I fired," Bob said. "Yeah, that's it."

"Good luck with the governor, boys," Clint said. "He's probably more of a crook then Frank and Jesse James ever were."

"Hey, Adams!" Bob shouted as Clint left. "Adams!"

"Did that accomplish anything?" Sheriff Timberlake asked as Clint strapped his gun back on.

"Nope."

"Then why do it?"

Clint looked at the man.

"Didn't know it wasn't going to accomplish anything when I thought of it, Sheriff. Where's Zee?"

"She went outside," Timberlake said. "Fine-looking woman."

"And strong, too," Clint said. "Strong, strong-willed, and smart."

"So you're tellin' me that if she wants the Fords dead, it can happen?"

"It can always happen, Sheriff," Clint said, "even right here—and whoever's with them might get it, too."

"Well," Timberlake said, "if Frank ain't gonna rise to the bait I don't reckon there's any reason to keep them here anymore."

"Somehow," Clint said, "I don't think that's going to be your decision. Good luck, Sheriff."

FORTY

Clint found Zee waiting outside.

"I want to kill them."

"I know."

She looked at him.

"I don't just want them dead," she said. "I want to kill them myself."

"I know. Come on, I'll walk you back to the house."

"I can walk myself."

"Zee, the people in this town—"

"I'm not ashamed of who Jesse was, Clint."

"I didn't say you were."

"I'll walk by myself," she said. "No one will bother me."

"All right."

Her hardened expression softened for just a moment and she said, "Thanks for bringing me here."

"I'm not sure I did you any good, Zee."

"Just the same," she said. "Thanks."

He nodded and watched as she walked down the street. She drew plenty of stares, but no one approached her, or spoke to her.

Clint went back to his hotel and sat in his room, thinking things over. What would they all do—Crittenden, Craig,

Timberlake, Pinkerton—now that he'd told them Frank wasn't coming into town? Would they take out after him? Wait and see if he formed his own James gang? Would they ship the Fords out before Clint had to meet with Frank again and tell him his "plan"?

And who could he get this information from?

Only one name came to mind.

He left his hotel and went in search of that person.

Just when he was starting to think the man had left town, he found him in one of the smaller saloons. As Clint approached the table, the Pinkerton man, Carl Burns, started to rise. Clint put his hand on the man's shoulder and pushed him back down.

"Hello, Carl."

"I ain't done nothin'," Burns said. "I gave your message to Pinkerton. It ain't my fault if he don't listen."

"What are you still doing in town, Carl?"

"I got fired," Burns grumbled.

"Oh, was that my fault?"

"Probably," Burns said. "When I told him you were here he got real mad. He fired me by return telegram. I don't even have a ticket home."

"Are there other Pinkertons in town now, Carl?" Clint asked.

"Guess there ain't no harm in tellin' you," the man said. "I don't work for them no more."

"No, you don't," Clint said. He realized that the man was more than a little drunk. "And since you're unemployed you probably don't have all that much money for drinks either. Why don't you let me buy you one, to try to make up for whatever part I had in getting you fired?"

"Don't know if you can make it up," Burns said, "but I'll take a drink."

"Whiskey?"

"This here's rotgut whiskey," Burns said, staring down at his glass.

"Don't even finish that, Carl," Clint said. "I'm going to get us a bottle of the good stuff. You wait right here."

"I ain't goin' nowhere," Burns said.

They worked on the bottle of good whiskey, Clint having a glass to every three Carl Burns had. By the time they had the level halfway down, Burns was acting like they were buddies, and that's what Clint wanted.

"So, you were in on the whole plan," Clint said to Burns.

"Right from the beginning," Burns blustered. "After all, I was the first one here, wasn't I? I spotted you here, didn't I?"

"You sure did."

"Then Pinkerton decides to work with the governor and send in more men, detectives *and* marshals, to catch Frank James."

"Only now Frank's not coming into St. Joe," Clint said.

Burns frowned and stared at Clint.

"He's not?"

"No."

"Hmph, ain't that a kick in the head?"

"So what will they do now?" Clint asked.

"Huh?"

"Now that Frank's not coming in," Clint repeated, very slowly, "what will the plan be now?"

"The plan?"

"There must be a backup plan."

Burns continued to frown, then brightened and said, "Oh, the contingency plan."

"That's right," Clint said, "the contingency plan."

"Well, tha's easy." He was slurring his words more now.

Clint waited, then said, "What's easy? What are they going to do?"

"They're gonna go get 'im."

"And how are they going to do that?"

"Well, he's in the area, ain't he?" Burns asked. "And they've got lots of men. They're jus' gonna . . . go get 'im."

"Carl—"

"Tired," Burns said, and put his head down on the table. He was asleep in seconds.

FORTY-ONE

The next morning Clint was sitting in a chair in front of the hotel. From his vantage point he could see the front of the jail. Well into the afternoon there was activity, men going in and out, but the Fords never appeared. Apparently, they were still trying to decide whether or not they had to go to their contingency plan.

By late afternoon all the comings and goings had stopped. Clint got up from the chair and walked over to the jail. When he entered he found Sheriff Timberlake seated behind his desk.

"What now?" the sheriff asked.

"I just came over for a talk," Clint said, sitting across from the man.

"About what?"

"Plans."

"What plans?"

"The plans that have been discussed all morning and afternoon. See, I've been sitting in front of the hotel all that time. You've had a lot of people in and out of here. My guess is you're being told what to do."

"What's so new about that?" Timberlake asked.

"Sheriff, I believe that you're not happy about what's happened."

"So? What does that earn me?"

"A chance to atone, maybe."

"Atone? How?"

Clint sat forward in his chair and stared across the desk at the man.

"By helping me save Frank James."

"You're crazy."

"Maybe not. . . ."

Clint's next stop was the telegraph office. He sent off a telegram to his friend Rick Hartman, who lived in Labyrinth Texas. He told the clerk to bring the answer to the Howard house.

"Jesse James's house?" the clerk asked nervously.

"Thomas Howard's house," Clint said. "Leave the reply with Mrs. Howard. Understand?"

"Yes, sir."

Clint leaned forward and stared directly into the clerk's eyes.

"And if I were you, I'd take down that reply without reading it. Get my meaning?"

The clerk swallowed and said, "Yes, sir."

"Do you think Frank will go for it?" Zee asked.

"Funny," Clint said, "I came here to ask you that."

"I don't know, Clint," she said, rubbing her arms as if she were cold. "It would mean forgetting about the Fords."

"For now, maybe—and maybe the Fords will get theirs down the line, somewhere."

"I want them to get theirs now."

"I'm trying to save Frank's life, Zee," Clint said. "You don't want him to end up like Jesse, do you?"

She didn't answer.

"Do you want his wife and son to end up like you?"

After a moment she said, "No, no, I don't. All right, I'll get a message to Frank."

"I'm waiting for a reply to a telegram from a friend," he

told her. ''If the clerk can't find me he's going to bring it here.''

''All right. I'll hold it for you. What are you going to do?''

''I'm going to find out who's in charge and talk to them,'' Clint said. ''I want to get this over with, for all our sakes.''

FORTY-TWO

From Timberlake Clint had found out who was in charge of the combined force of marshals and detectives who were in town. His name was Captain John Breck, although Clint had no idea what he was captain of.

He found Breck in the Red Branch Saloon, one of the smaller establishments in town. It offered no gambling or women, just drinks.

Breck was seated at a back table. He was a tall, broad-shouldered man with shoulder-length hair, and the way he sat behind the table it was almost as if he were sitting at a desk. As Clint approached he saw the lines in the man's face. From the door Breck looked forty; closer inspection put him over fifty.

"Captain Breck?"

The man had nothing in front of him but a mug of beer, yet he seemed to be studying something on the table. He looked up from it slowly.

"Mr. Adams, have a seat."

"You know me?" Clint asked as he sat.

"I know of you, sir," Breck said, "and yes, I have seen you before."

"I'm sorry," Clint said, "but if we've met before—"

"I didn't say we'd met," Breck said, cutting him off, "just that I had seen you before."

"Are you a marshal, Captain Breck, or—"

"I have the honor of working for Mr. Allan Pinkerton."

"I see . . . and the rank? Captain?"

"I was a captain during the war."

The war had been over for a long time, but Clint didn't comment on that.

"What can I do for you, Mr. Adams?"

"You can call off your dogs."

"I'm sorry," Breck said, "my dogs?"

"Your men, your combined forces," Clint said. "Frank James will be giving himself up soon."

"Is that a fact?"

"It is," Clint said. It was a lie, of course. He still had to talk Frank into his "plan."

"And for that reason you think that we should all just pack up and go home?"

"I would hope you would."

"Well, sir," Breck said, "you hope in vain. Oh, rest assured I shall telegraph Mr. Pinkerton and give him this news, but I doubt that he will tell me to . . . take my 'dogs' and go home."

"I think you'll find that the marshals will be pulling out," Clint said. If, he didn't add, Rick Hartman was able to pull off some magic through his many contacts.

"That may be the case," Breck said, "but I will abide by what my employer tells me."

"I see," Clint said, "you've become more accustomed to taking orders than giving them."

"You are attempting to . . . get my goat? Is that the metaphor? Since we're using animal metaphors, here. You won't succeed. I think our conversation is through."

"Frank's going to come in on his own," Clint said, standing. "You tell Allan I said that, and that I'll be with him."

"Oh, I'll tell him," Breck said. "He'll find it very interesting, I'm sure."

Breck was arrogant, as evidenced by his continuous use of his war rank well after the war was over. He and Allan Pinkerton were perfect for each other.

There was no need for Rick Hartman's telegram to be delivered to "Thomas Howard's" house, and for this the clerk was very grateful. As he left the telegraph office he spotted Clint walking toward his hotel.

"Mr. Adams?"

Clint turned, saw the clerk, and waited.

"Here's your reply from Texas, sir," the clerk said, handing it to him.

"Thank you."

"I, uh, have already forgotten it," the clerk said, and ran back to the office.

Actually, there was nothing to forget. It said: STRINGS PULLED. YOU OWE ME. It was signed RICK HARTMAN.

FORTY-THREE

They met in a clearing well out of town, and away from the caves. Frank was smart enough to stay away from them for a while.

"All right," Frank said without preamble as Clint arrived, "what's your plan?"

"You won't like it right away," Clint said, "but I'd like you to take the time to consider it."

"What is it?"

"Turn yourself in."

Frank didn't answer.

"I've already taken steps to get to the governor."

"What steps?"

"A friend of mine who has contacts has pulled some strings."

"What evidence is there of this?"

"The marshals will be gone from St. Joe by morning."

Frank looked impressed.

"What about the Pinkertons?"

"You know Allan Pinkerton's character as well as I do," Clint said. "What will he do?"

"Balk," Frank said. "Be stubborn."

"Right."

"So where would we do this?"

Was Frank actually considering it?

"Jefferson City, right on the steps of the City Hall. You'll hand your gun to the governor."

"In return for what?"

"Amnesty."

"Total amnesty?"

Clint hesitated, then said, "That's still to be worked out."

Frank dropped his horse's reins to the ground and walked around a bit, considering.

"Frank, I have to say I'm surprised you're considering this."

"Why'd you come up with it if you thought I wouldn't go along with it?"

"I was hoping to talk you into it."

"The truth is," Frank said, "I've been thinking about it myself, for some time."

"You have?"

"What you said the other night about Jesse maybe not being the smartest sort of sunk in. You see, Jesse would never consider this. Jesse would go after the Fords until he got them or died trying."

"But not you."

"I have a wife and a young son," Frank said. "Amnesty sounds pretty good right now, Clint."

"The details need to be ironed out. You might even have to stand trial."

"Like the Fords?"

"Yes, like the Fords."

"Tell me," Frank said, "have you talked to them?"

"I have."

"And how has their deal with the governor worked out?"

"Not well," Clint said, "but you have something they didn't."

"What's that?"

"Me."

Frank paced around some more, and Clint gave him time to think.

"Having you on my side in the past has always worked out, Clint," he said finally. "You see what you can do about working this out. I'll be in touch."

"Don't come into town, Frank," Clint said. "I think I've gotten rid of the marshals, but the Pinkertons are still around. They're being led by a Captain Breck, who sounds as stubborn as ol' Allan."

"I won't come in," Frank said, "until I hear from you."

"You won't regret this, Frank."

"I hope not," Frank said, as they shook hands, "because if I do, so will you."

FORTY-FOUR

Rick Hartman's contact was the friend of a man who knew a man who was a fairly powerful politician in Washington. Since T. T. Crittenden had ambitions to be a "Washington" politician he "listened" when the man in power sent him a telegram saying that it might be a good idea—and a good career move—to grant Frank James amnesty.

When Clint got back to St. Joe he noticed that all the marshals were gone, already. This was the first thing that Crittenden had to do.

He also noticed that the Pinkertons were still in town, and still very much in evidence. These were not Pinkertons like his friend Talbot Roper had been a Pinkerton. Roper was a detective, and these were bullyboys, or bounty hunters.

As he rode Duke down the main street of St. Joe to the livery, he could feel the eyes on him. The hard stares he was getting from these Pinkertons were almost like forefingers poking him in the back.

He rode Duke into the livery and took care of him by himself. He unsaddled him, rubbed him down, and fed him. When he turned to leave he was looking at four men, all of a kind, the "bullyboy" kind. They had well-worn guns on. These were the weapons of their choice, and they were comfortable with them. Their clothes, however, were fairly new, bought with Pinkerton money.

"Can I help you boys?"

"We know what you're tryin' to do," one of the men said.

"And what am I trying to do?"

"Tryin' to get Frank James off," the man said.

"Tryin' to get him to turn himself in," another said.

"Tryin' to take food out of our mouths," a third said.

Clint stared at the fourth man, who appeared to have nothing to say.

"You boys are biting off a little more than you can chew here," Clint said. "Did Breck send you over? *Captain* Breck? He hasn't been a captain for a long time, has he? He sent you here to warn me, or kill me? What? Beat me up?"

"Make a point," the first man said.

"Well, make it and walk out of here."

"We'll make it," the man said, "and we'll walk out, but you won't."

"It'll be a while before you can walk out of here," the second man said.

"And even then you'll be limping," the third man said.

Clint looked at the fourth man, who had nothing to say. He was taller than the others, thinner, wearing a full beard, and he had tiny eyes. This was the one he had to worry about, Clint decided. This was the one he'd kill first, the one who didn't talk.

"You boys are making a mistake if you think I'm going to stand here and let you maim me."

"The alternative is to make us kill you," the first man said.

"You'd do better to take the beatin' like a man."

"You gotta—" the third man said, but Clint had heard enough.

"Get out of my way."

He took a step forward, something the four men weren't ready for. They would have understood if he'd stepped back, but coming toward them, that confused them.

"Wait—" the first man said.

That was when the fourth man moved. His hand streaked for his gun, and Clint could tell he was good. If the others had been anywhere near as good as this man he would have been in trouble.

Clint shot the fourth man before he could bring his gun up. The tiny eyes reflected his surprise as the bullet struck him in the chest.

Clint turned quickly and shot the first man in the knee. He went down with a scream, clutching at the wound, blood streaming from between his fingers.

"Anybody else?" he asked.

The other two men, who had made no moves for their guns, were stunned, and held their hands up, away from their guns.

"Then get out of my way."

They did so. Clint started forward, then stopped and looked down at the first man.

"You didn't . . . have to . . . do that . . ." the man gasped.

"Yes," Clint said, "I did."

FORTY-FIVE

Captain Breck tried to have Clint arrested the next day for killing one of his men and crippling another, but Timberlake wouldn't go along with it. Neither would Commissioner Craig, who had already heard from Governor Crittenden. Craig came to St. Joe and, with Timberlake, went to Clint's hotel. When Clint opened the door to his room and saw them he said, "Wait for me downstairs. I'll be down in a minute."

He closed the door in their faces.

When he came down to the lobby both men were waiting. He could see by the look on Craig's face that the man was annoyed.

"Adams, I'm Commissioner Craig."

"I know who you are," Clint said. "Why are you here?"

"To arrange for the surrender of Frank James," Craig said. "He's to surrender to me here—"

"Frank will surrender to the governor on the steps of the capitol building," Clint said. "You arrange the when, but that's where and how. He'll hand Governor T. T. Crittenden his guns, as long as he's assured he'll be treated fairly."

"He'll have to stand trial."

"Fair trial," Clint said.

"Of course," Craig blustered. He was Timberlake's age but much better dressed. He wore a vested suit with an expensive watch dangling from—or lying on—his oversized belly. "I'll need to talk to Frank James."

"You talk to me," Clint said. "When the arrangements are made I'll bring him in."

"This is outrageous—"

"This is the way it will be," Clint said. "This will be a big help to the governor's career—and maybe even to yours."

Craig frowned, not liking it, but then thinking it over and apparently agreeing with Clint.

"Very well," Commissioner Craig said, "I'll make the arrangements."

"You get back to me with the time," Clint said, "and we'll be there."

"Very well."

As Craig turned to leave, Clint said, "Commissioner."

"Yes?"

"No marshals or deputies," Clint said, "and no Pinkertons. I'll shoot the first man who tries to reach for a gun. Is that understood?"

"It's understood," Craig said. "I don't know how you did this, or who you know in Washington, but it's understood."

Clint watched as the two lawmen left the hotel and knew he was going to owe Rick Hartman a big one after this.

EPILOGUE

On the evening of October 5 Clint and Frank James rode into Jefferson City and proceeded directly to the capitol building. As they dismounted they could see Governor T. T. Crittenden waiting at the top of the steps. There were some men with him, but they were unarmed.

"Who are they?" Frank asked.

"Aides," Clint said. "Don't worry. He'll keep his word to us, not like with the Fords."

"I like that," Frank said. "Should piss those boys off."

Together they mounted the steps, and Clint was on the lookout for trouble. It would be unlike Allan Pinkerton not to try something.

When they reached the top of the steps Frank James and the Governor of Missouri stared at each other. Finally, Frank unbuckled his gun belt and handed it to the governor, who looked down at the Remington .44 caliber revolver and forty-two rounds of ammunition.

"Governor," Frank said, "for the first time in twenty-one years I allow another man to take my pistol, and it's the happiest day of my life." Frank went on with a speech he had prepared, one that Clint had been listening to the entire way, on the trail. Frank had told him that this should be a memorable day.

"I have trusted you as I have never trusted another man," Frank finished. "Do with me what you will."

The governor was touched by Frank's speech.

"You will have all the protection the law can offer," he said, "and the fair trial you were promised."

At that moment several men stepped forward. They were marshals, Clint could see, but they were unarmed.

It was arranged that Frank would go to Independence, Missouri, in the company of the governor's secretary, F. C. Farr. They were to leave at midnight. Until then Frank went to stay at the house of a family named McCarty, where a thousand people filed in to shake his hand. Clint stayed also, and was amazed at how the people of Jefferson City seemed to love Frank.

Later Clint, Frank, and Farr got on the train to Independence. When they arrived they were met by Commissioner Craig, a prosecuting attorney named Wallace, and a marshal named Murphy, who had three warrants for Frank's arrest. He was charged with the murder of the Pinkerton agent, Whicher; the Rocky Cut robbery; and a murder and holdup in Winston.

Clint knew then that Pinkerton wasn't around because Frank had been charged with the murder of his man. It was probably the governor's concession to Allan Pinkerton to keep him out of the way.

Frank turned, shook hands with Clint, and was taken away.

In the days and months ahead Frank James was tried three times, and found not guilty three times by a jury of his peers. Minnesota had intended to charge him and try him for his part in the Northfield bank holdup, but they decided it wasn't worth the effort. They couldn't get him tried outside of Missouri, and no jury in Missouri would convict him. He would live out his life as a legend and die of a heart attack in 1915.

Under the constant fear that Frank James would find them and kill them, Charley Ford, two years after helping his brother kill Jesse James, committed suicide.

Bob Ford lived until 1892, when a man just about shot his head off with a shotgun following an argument.

After leaving Frank in Independence—where his wife and child had come to be with him—Clint went back to St. Joe to say good-bye to Zee. Neither of them acknowledged what had happened between them one night in a hotel room in Kearney, but likewise neither of them would forget.

They would never see each other again.

BIBLIOGRAPHY

The Day Jesse James Was Killed, Carl Breihan, Signet, 1961, 1979.

The Gunfighter: Man or Myth?, Joseph G. Rosa, Oklahoma Press, 1969.

Outlaws of the Old West, Carl Breihan, Roger M. McBride Co., 1957, Signet, 1980.

The Pinkertons: The Detective Dynasty that Made History, James D. Horan, Bonanza, 1968.

AUTHOR'S NOTE

Certain liberties have been taken with the dates of some of the incidents described in this book. Likewise, liberties have been taken with the age of Duke, the Gunsmith's big black gelding. Please, don't anyone write telling us that Clint could not possibly have gotten Duke the way he did because the dates of the incidents and the age of the horse don't jibe. This is fiction, and it all jibes if I want it to.

And if you'll let it.

J. R. Roberts

Watch for

THE GAMBLER

201st novel in the exciting GUNSMITH series
from Jove

Coming in October!